Nothing like a brush with death to get your priorities straight.

Callie wasn't interested in whatever drama between her and Harlan . . . all that was more like trivial nonsense. Right now, she had to worry about getting the killers behind bars.

Still, she had to admit that when she'd heard Harlan's voice calling to her from beneath the rubble of the landslide, the relief she'd felt had been palpable. The sudden fear of losing him had ripped through her like a dark tide.

Did that mean she was still in love with him? So be it. But she couldn't let that interfere with what they'd come here to do.

Harlan seemed to be feeling the same way. He'd gotten quiet again as they rode the trail. He'd taken the lead now, and his focus and determination was a comfort to her.

It was also, she realized as her heartbeat galloped, an undeniable aphrodisiac.

ALANA MATTHEWS

A WANTED MAN

TORONTO NEW YORK LONDON
AMSTERDAM PARIS SYDNEY HAMBURG
STOCKHOLM ATHENS TOKYO MILAN MADRID
PRAGUE WARSAW BUDAPEST AUCKLAND

Recycling programs
for this product may
not exist in your area.

ISBN-13: 978-0-373-74660-6

A WANTED MAN

Copyright © 2012 by Alana Matthews

ABOUT THE AUTHOR

Alana Matthews can't remember a time when she didn't want to be a writer. As a child, she was a permanent fixture in her local library, and she soon turned her passion for books into writing short stories, and finally novels. A longtime fan of romance suspense, Alana felt she had no choice but to try her hand at the genre, and she is thrilled to be writing for Harlequin Intrigue. Alana makes her home in a small town near the coast of Southern California, where she spends her time writing, composing music and watching her favorite movies. Send a message to Alana at her website, www.alanamatthews.com.

Books by Alana Matthews

HARLEQUIN INTRIGUE
1208—MAN UNDERCOVER
1239—BODY ARMOR
1271—WATERFORD POINT
1339—A WANTED MAN

CAST OF CHARACTERS

Deputy Sheriff Callie Glass—A clue found at the scene of a heinous crime brought her face-to-face with her past.

Deputy U.S. Marshal Harlan Cole—His mistake could have cost him his life, but instead brought him straight back into Callie's.

Nana Jean—Callie's no-nonsense grandmother, who raised Callie and made no bones about interfering with her love life.

Landry Bickham—He always had a smile on his face, but behind it was the brain of a reptile.

Deputy Rusty Wilcox—A deputy training under Callie's supervision, too often caught in the crossfire when sparks flew between Callie and Harlan.

Gloria Pritchard-Breen—A bitter, wounded woman who holds a grudge against Callie.

Jonah Pritchard—A descendant of outlaws who thought the best solution was often one that required a shotgun.

Billy Boy Lyman—A fugitive from justice who would do anything to keep from being caught.

Megan Prichard-Breen—A young sociopath who got her kicks running around with bad boys like Billy.

Sheriff Mercer—A tough boss whose life got tougher when he hit the trail to catch a fugitive.

Chapter One

"I gotta make a pit stop," Billy Boy said.

U.S. Deputy Marshal Harlan Cole sighed and glanced at his prisoner in the rearview mirror. It was one thing after another with this guy, and he was tired of listening to him.

Billy Boy Lyman had spent half the drive moaning about his cuffs being too tight, the cruiser being too cold, then he started blathering on about how the courts and the Marshals Service had him all wrong. That he was an innocent man caught up in something way over his head.

When Harlan reminded him that he'd tried to rob a bank, put a gun in the teller's face and threatened to pull the trigger, Billy said, "My *partners* were the ones with the guns. I didn't even wanna *be* there—you know?"

"Uh-huh," Harlan muttered, then spent the next two hours listening to Billy Boy's tale of woe, the majority of which was little more than a sorry attempt at justifying the commission of a very serious crime.

Now, true to form, he was making noise about having to "pick a daisy," as Aunt Maggie used to say.

"I'm serious," Billy told him. "I really gotta go."

"Can't it wait until we get to Torrington?"

"Not unless you wanna be mopping up this backseat."

Harlan sighed again and looked out at the night sky and the empty road rolling under his headlights. He had picked Lyman up at the Criminal Justice Center in Colorado Springs, after waiting the good part of an hour for the prisoner to be processed. It had been a long day and all he wanted was to get the man squared away, then head to his motel room and go to bed.

He just wished Billy Boy would shut up. A wish that was likely to go unfulfilled.

This all came with the job, of course. Harlan knew that. The U.S. Marshals Service specialized in fugitive retrieval and prisoner transport, and he'd spent a significant amount of his career chauffeuring dimwits from one jail cell to another. He figured he'd probably heard just about every lamebrained excuse a man could come up with for breaking the law, and normally he wasn't much affected by it. Took it all in stride.

But there was something about Billy Boy that rubbed him the wrong way. The kid couldn't have been more than twenty-two years old, but he had one of those smirky little faces you just wanted to put a fist in. It took every bit of Harlan's impulse control to stop himself from pulling to the side of the highway to give the kid a quick tune-up.

On nights like this Harlan wondered if he should've taken his father's advice and found a different line of work. His father had been a career deputy and when Harlan had decided to follow in his footsteps, the old man had groaned.

"You've got smarts, boy. Use that big brain of yours to make a difference in the world."

But Harlan figured he *was* making a difference. There was nothing more satisfying than taking down a fugitive and helping ensure that the world was a better, safer place. It was just that he sometimes felt as if he were little more than a cattle herder. Even if the livestock he dealt with had a dangerous streak.

Not that Billy Boy was all that dangerous. Just annoying. And the sooner he delivered him to the Wyoming Medium Correctional Institution, the happier he'd be.

"Are we gonna make a stop or what?" Billy asked. "And I ain't talkin' about the side of the road. I like my privacy, and there's bound to be a gas station up ahead."

Harlan glanced at his prisoner in the rearview mirror. "Only on one condition."

"Which is?"

"After you've done your business, you shut your yap and keep it shut for the rest of the ride."

THE CONVENIENCE STORE was one of those all-nighters with a couple of gas pumps out front. It stood just off the highway, the only sign of life in the vicinity, its fluorescent lights so bright you could see them from half a mile away beckoning late night travelers to stop in for a snack, a cup of coffee and a few gallons of gas.

It was close to midnight and Harlan wasn't surprised to find only a single car parked out front—a battered gray Chevy Malibu he recognized as one that had passed them a few miles back.

Harlan wasn't fond of making unscheduled stops, but he understood how merciless the call of nature could sometimes be. When he worked long transports like this one, he tended to cut back on his liquid intake, but there wasn't much he could do about his passenger. It was up to the previous custodian to make sure the prisoner had been properly "fed and bled" before the trip. Yet despite the long processing time, someone back in Colorado Springs had neglected to do his job.

Harlan parked two slots over from the Chevy, then killed the engine and turned, staring at Billy Boy through the grille that separated the front and backseats.

"You'll wanna watch your step in there. Even a hint of trouble and I *will* shoot you. You understand?"

Lyman smirked. "You ever shot a prisoner before?"

"Once," Harlan said. "And he looked a lot like you."

The smirk disappeared. "You got nothing to worry about with me, Marshal. Like I told you, I'm an innocent man."

"Uh-huh."

Harlan popped his door open and climbed out. Resting the palm of his right hand on the butt of the Glock holstered at his hip, he moved to the back and pulled open the passenger door.

With his own hands cuffed behind him, Billy Boy had to struggle a bit to climb out of the cruiser, but he managed to do it without too much of a fuss. Then Harlan took hold of his arm and guided him toward the convenience store entrance.

When they got inside, Harlan was surprised to find a woman—a girl, really— behind the counter. Places like this tended to hire males for the late shift on the belief that a lone female offered any potential troublemakers a more vulnerable target.

But this particular female didn't look even remotely vulnerable. In fact, despite her youth and obvious beauty, there was a defiance in her expression that was a little offputting. A look that said, *mess with me and find out*. She probably had a loaded piece resting somewhere under that counter, just in case the class got unruly.

Harlan saw her hackles rise as a buzzer announced their arrival and they came through the door, her gaze immediately shifting to Billy Boy's cuffed hands.

He didn't bother explaining the obvious,

and didn't waste any time with chitchat, either. "Restroom?"

A guy in the potato chip aisle at the back of the store—the driver of the Malibu, no doubt—looked up at the sound of Harlan's voice. He glanced curiously at the man wearing cuffs, then went back to minding his own business.

Harlan waited as the girl reached under the counter and brought out a key attached to a wooden paddle. He'd always thought that the necessity for such things was a pretty sad commentary on the state of the world, but he took it from her without comment, then moved in the direction of her pointed finger toward a hallway just to her left.

The hallway was small and cramped with a single door marked Toilet. Harlan shoved the key into the lock, then pushed the door open and gestured Billy Boy inside.

Billy frowned. "Ain't you gonna take these cuffs off?"

"Once we're inside," Harlan said.

Billy looked surprised. "*We?* You're gonna watch me do my business? I *told* you, I like my privacy."

"My mandate is to keep you in sight at all times, whether I like it or not. You seem to be under the mistaken impression that I should trust you."

"What do you think I'm gonna do? Whack you with my—"

"Just get inside, Billy. I've had about all I can tolerate of you. The sooner we're done here, the better off we'll both be."

"You ain't exactly Officer Friendly, are you?"

"Sorry to disappoint. Now let's get this over with."

Billy Boy scowled but did as he was told, stepping into a room about the size of a broom closet that sported a single toilet and sink. There wasn't enough room inside for both of them, so Harlan moved forward and uncuffed his prisoner, then stepped back and waited in the open doorway.

"You ain't gonna close the door?"

"I'm gonna close your mouth with my fist if you don't hurry it up."

"All right, all right," Billy said, stepping up to the toilet. "Don't get your panties in a wad." He turned his head slightly. "Speaking of which, what do you think of that counter girl? Kinda cute, huh?"

"I think she's way out of your league."

"Yeah? I bet if I treated her right, she'd do anything I told her."

Harlan almost laughed. "Dream on, Billy. Now will you please get to it already? I'd really like to—"

Harlan froze as something cold and metallic touched the back of his head.

"Hands behind your neck," a voice said.

A female voice.

Damn.

Harlan didn't have to see her face to know it was the aforementioned counter girl. He also didn't have to use that big brain of his to figure out that she wasn't a counter girl at all. She'd no doubt been riding in the battered Chevy Malibu parked outside, along with the potato chip lover. And chances were pretty good that the *real* counter girl—or more likely *man*—was either dead or tied up in a closet somewhere.

Harlan inwardly cursed himself. He'd been at this job for nearly ten years now and he'd just pulled a rookie move. Let the prisoner lull him—or, in this case, *annoy* him—into lowering his guard.

How could he be so stupid?

"Hands," the girl said again. "Now."

As Harlan sighed and laced his fingers

behind his neck, Billy Boy Lyman turned around, that infuriating smirk once again adorning his face. He reached forward and removed Harlan's Glock from its holster.

"You were right not to trust me," he said.

Then he brought the gun up fast, slamming it into the side of Harlan's head.

Chapter Two

They found the burned-out shell of the pickup truck parked on the side of the highway about forty miles south of Williamson. It was still smoldering when a highway patrol officer pulled off the road behind it, thinking it was just another abandoned vehicle whose owner had gotten a little carried away.

As soon as he took a closer look, however, he discovered it hadn't been abandoned after all.

There was a body inside.

The medical examiner on scene had warned Callie that what she was about to see would not be pleasant—what people in the trade referred to as a *crispy critter*. And true enough, the sight of that blackened lump on the front seat was one she knew she'd be spending the next couple weeks trying to bleach from her brain.

Despite the damage, the truck's rear license tag had been spared—an oasis amidst a desolate landscape—and when she called it in, she found out the pickup belonged to none other than Jim Farber, a local rancher.

Considering the fact that Farber hadn't been seen since yesterday morning, the logical conclusion was that *he* was the lump on the front seat.

Callie wouldn't know for certain until forensics did its thing, but she was a strong believer in Occam's razor—that the simplest explanation was the most likely one. After seven years with the Williamson County Sheriff's Department, working crimes a lot more complicated than this, she'd come to rely on that dictum as if it were gospel.

The question, as always, was who had done this and why? Williamson, Wyoming, wasn't exactly known for its violent crime, and the handful of murders Callie had investigated in the course of her career usually led her straight to a member of the victim's family.

That, however, didn't seem to be the case here. Only careful examination would determine the actual cause of death, but whatever it might be, Callie couldn't imagine Farber's wife or either of their two kids pouring gasoline over the family truck and setting it on fire. This was a dispassionate crime, and the Farbers were anything but. It was certainly possible that Callie was wrong about that, but she didn't think so.

A groan pulled her out of her thoughts. "I think I'm gonna be sick," Rusty said, clutching his stomach, his face a couple shades whiter than it had been when they'd pulled up in their SUV a few moments ago.

Rusty Wilcox was a good number of years younger than Callie and hadn't been on the job long enough to build immunity against sights like this. Even Callie was finding it more difficult than usual to shut her mind off to the horror of it all.

But she couldn't let Rusty know this. She was his training deputy, breaking him into the cold, cruel reality of the sheriff's Major Crimes Squad, and it was important to maintain her professionalism at all times.

This wasn't much of a struggle for her, however. Over the years she'd learned to bottle up her emotions, a trait that had soured quite a few relationships.

The truth was, *she* was the dispassionate one. And at thirty-four, she had come to the conclusion that she was destined to spend the rest of her life flying solo. She no longer embraced the dream of a husband and kids and a white picket fence.

She looked at Rusty and could see that he was struggling to hold back the blueberry muffin he'd gobbled up on the ride over, despite her warning that what he was about to see wouldn't be pretty.

"Do it on the other side of the road," she said tersely. "You don't want to contaminate the crime scene."

As Rusty stumbled across the blacktop, Callie went back to her thoughts only to have them interrupted again by a shout from the far side of the pickup truck.

"Deputy Glass! I think I've found something."

She glanced at Rusty, then moved around toward the source of the shout and found one of her crime scene techs crouched next to the passenger door—a grinning, gap-toothed kid named Tucker Davies.

Why did everyone around Callie seem to be getting younger these days?

"Check this out," he said, excitement lighting his eyes as he pointed to a spot just under the truck.

Callie hunkered down and looked. Saw a lump of half-melted polymer that roughly formed the shape of a handgun. A forty caliber Glock from the looks of it. Just like the one she carried.

Callie immediately understood Tucker's excitement. "Let's just pray the serial number is intact."

"Only one way to find out."

Tucker reached a gloved hand under the truck and carefully picked up the weapon. He pulled it out, studied it, then showed Callie the trigger guard which looked relatively unscathed. "Only a partial, but it might be enough."

This was turning out to be a good day for numbers. First the license tag, now this. And maybe the question of *who* and *why* would be answered much more quickly than Callie had dared hope.

"Let's get it into the system as soon as possible. Hit every database you can think of. I want to know who owns that weapon."

"Might take a while," Tucker told her.

"Then I guess you'd better get started."

WILLIAMSON COUNTY Sheriff's Deputy Callie Glass was a Wyoming native, born and bred.

She'd drawn her first breath on a cold Thursday morning in her mother's bedroom. Her mother was eighteen years old and barely out of high school, screaming in agony as she pushed her first and only child into the world, then promptly passed on.

Some said that Callie's mom might have survived if she'd been in a proper hospital and hadn't been victim to an inexperienced midwife. But there was no way to know that for sure. The hemorrhaging had come on swift and without warning, and the poor girl was dead within minutes of the delivery. Besides, Mary Glass was a free spirit who had never trusted hospitals, and wouldn't have poked so much as a toe inside one—even if her life *had* depended on it.

Callie's father was a kid named Riley Pritchard, who had enlisted in the army a week after he'd found out young Mary was pregnant. The Pritchards were one of the richest families in Williamson, and there was no doubt in anyone's mind that Riley's father, Jonah, had nudged the boy into action, hoping to avoid the possibility of a bastard child claiming heir to their precious family fortune.

By the time Callie was born, Riley had

been killed when a base supply struck over-turned and crushed him, so the only parent she'd ever known was the woman she called Nana Jean.

Despite being widowed and borderline destitute, Nana had stepped up to the challenge of raising an infant and had done it without complaint.

Most of the time.

What few complaints Nana *did* have, came much later in Callie's life, after a string of romantic disasters had made it clear that her granddaughter's spirit wasn't easily tamed, a trait she had inherited from her mother.

"I just wish you'd settle down," the old woman often told Callie. "Find yourself somebody to share your life with. I won't be around to hold your hand forever."

But Callie was defiant. "Who says it needs holding?"

"Listen, child, you can be the most inde-pendent woman on the face of earth, but you still need a little romance in your life. It's been far too long."

"So why didn't *you* ever get married again?"

"Your grandfather was one of a kind. Any man tried to replace him would only wind up heartbroken, and I'm not about to do that to someone."

"He must've been pretty special."

Nana nodded, a wistful look in her eyes. She'd never been a sentimental woman, so Callie knew that what she was about to say was sincere. "This'll sound like a lie, but I swear to you that up until the day he died, my heart would flutter every time Walter walked into the room."

Callie smiled. "That's sweet."

"Yes, it is, and I keep hoping you'll find someone who does that to *you*. I thought you had it, once, but you're too stubborn to—"

"All right, Nana. I think we're done here."

This conversation was just a rehash of a dozen others they'd had over the past few years, Nana worried about Callie's ever-ticking clock. Such exchanges usually ended with Callie politely but firmly suggesting that Nana let her worry about her own love life. That she had more important things to think about, like putting bad guys in jail.

And *that,* she insisted, was about all the testosterone she was interested in dealing with these days.

"You go on, keep lying to yourself," Nana

would always say—a handful of words for which Callie had yet to find a suitable response.

No MATTER WHAT CASE she might be working on, Callie tried her best to go home for lunch every day, and today was no exception.

Once the crime scene was squared away and the evidence had been tagged and bagged, she dropped Rusty off at the station house with instructions to make sure Tucker Davies called her just as soon as he got a hit on the Glock.

Then she drove the mile and a half home, where she knew Nana would be waiting for her with a sandwich and a glass of iced tea.

Their usual routine was to sit and watch Nana's favorite soap. And as the melodrama played out on screen, Callie would invariably start thinking about how old and frail Nana was looking and worry that she might not be around long enough to see how the stories ended.

Today, however, as Callie pulled up to the curb, she was surprised to find a plumber's truck parked in their driveway. Which didn't make sense. They'd had the entire house repiped less than six months ago, and for the money they'd spent, there shouldn't be any need for an emergency visit. Besides, Callie herself usually handled such arrangements, and if there was a problem Nana would have called her.

But when she went inside, she found Nana and the plumber sitting in the front parlor, sharing a pitcher of tea, as if this were nothing more than a social visit.

Although he looked vaguely familiar—about Callie's age and marginally handsome, if you liked the type—she had no idea who this man might be.

Nana took care of that straightaway. "Cal, this is Judith's grandnephew Henry. He just moved to town and I thought it might be nice for him to drop by for a little refreshment."

The lightbulb suddenly went on and Callie remembered where she'd seen him before: in a photograph on Judith's mantel. Judith had been Nana's best friend since childhood.

Callie knew immediately what was going on here and forced a smile. "Hello, Henry, nice to meet you."

Henry got to his feet and shook her hand as Callie shifted her gaze to her grandmother. "Nana, can I speak to you for a moment?"

"Why don't you have a seat, dear? I'll pour you some tea."

"I think we need to talk alone."

Nana reluctantly rose from her chair and followed Callie into the kitchen. Callie could see that the old woman was bracing for a scolding, and she was all too happy to give her one.

As they passed through the doorway, she felt heat rising in her chest and struggled to keep her voice low. "What in God's name are you thinking?"

"He's a nice boy, dear. What's the harm in having him stop by for a glass of tea?"

"Is Judith in on this, too?"

Nana smiled. "Well, I guess she'd have to be, wouldn't she?"

"How many times have I told you, I can handle my own love life. I don't need you and Judith interfering."

"With what? You haven't had a date in six months."

Callie glared at her. "I mean it, Nana."

"Listen, hon, those pipes of yours must be just about frozen solid. Wouldn't hurt to have a handsome young plumber check 'em out. Who knows where it might lead?"

Callie felt her face grow red. "I can't believe you just said that."

"What—you think because I'm old I've forgotten what it's like to have a little—"

"Stop," Callie said, her voice louder and more shrill than she'd intended it to be. She did her best to calm herself. "Nana, I appreciate your concern, I really do, but please, stop trying to force the issue."

"Dear, if I don't force the issue, I'll be dead before—"

The ring of Callie's cell phone cut her off. Callie took it from her pocket and checked the screen: Tucker Davies.

Already?

That was fast.

She jabbed a button on the keypad and put the phone to her ear. "Tell me this is good news."

"Better than good," Tucker said. "Turns out the Glock has a custom serial number, just like the weapons *we* use, only this one's assigned to the U.S. Marshals Service."

"You've gotta be kidding me."

"I put in a call and found out that one of their deputies lost it last night when the prisoner he was transporting got the better of him. They were headed for Wyoming Correctional, coming up from Colorado Springs."

Callie felt her heartbeat quicken. That prisoner was more than likely her perpetrator. How he'd wound up in Jim Farber's truck was a mystery, but at least they knew who they were looking for.

"I need to talk to this deputy," she said.

"Shouldn't be a problem, since he's already in the vicinity. He's on his way to the station house as we speak."

"Oh? What's his name?"

"Cole," Davies said. "Deputy Harlan Cole."

Callie hesitated, certain she hadn't heard him right. "Say that again?"

He enunciated carefully. "Harlan...Cole."

His words were like a sledgehammer to Callie's chest. If she didn't know better, she'd swear her heart had suddenly stopped dead.

The name was not unfamiliar to her.

Far from it.

And the thought of Harlan Cole walking into her life after all these years made her want to turn and flee. If this was nature taking its course, then she wanted nothing to do with it.

Without warning a bucketful of memories flooded her mind. And while the pain that the name *Harlan Cole* invoked had long been relegated to a tiny corner of her brain, it now sprang forward as if freed from a cage, an untamed and ferocious beast, anxious to devour.

"Deputy Glass?"

Callie had to search for a moment, but finally found her voice. "Thanks, Tucker. I'm on my way."

As she disconnected, she realized Nana was staring at her, concern in her eyes. "What's the matter, hon? You okay?"

Far from it, Callie thought, knowing it would take every bit of her strength to climb into her SUV and drive back to the station house.

Because Deputy Harlan Cole wasn't just a U.S. Marshal. He was a man she had long despised.

He was also the love of her life.

Chapter Three

Harlan had no idea what to expect when he walked into the Williamson County Sheriff's Department.

He was feeling humiliated and out of sorts after last night's debacle, the side of his head still throbbing where Billy Boy Lyman had left a Glock-size bruise.

When he came to, he'd found himself lying in the restroom doorway, the room swaying, his weapon long gone. But what hurt most was the blow to his pride. In the span of less than a minute, he had lost a prisoner, a gun and a sizable chunk of his reputation. All because he'd been stupid enough to lower his guard, and was just biased enough to assume that the girl behind the counter wasn't a threat to him.

Something he'd have to work on.

Whatever the case, he didn't doubt that

these mistakes would haunt him for many months to come. And as he pulled into the Williamson County Sheriff's Office parking structure, he had no idea what he was walking into.

The locals would undoubtedly blame him for the death of one of their own, but the question was whether they'd take the professional route and hide their animosity, or—as was so often the case—treat him like a hostile intruder.

The moment he stepped into the conference room, however, such concerns immediately vacated his mind. This could have been a war zone, with bullets flying, and Harlan wouldn't have noticed.

Of the six people sitting at the long table, only one of them—the lone woman in the room—commanded his attention, despite the fact that she refused to look him directly in the eye.

It was none other than Callie Glass.

Harlan's internal alarm bells suddenly went off, and he knew he'd better sit down before he *fell* down. While he would've loved to have blamed his sudden disorientation on his head injury, that was only part of it. The sight of his old college flame sitting not ten feet away from him had thrown him completely off balance.

Was he imagining things? Had the bump on his noggin brought on some cruel hallucination?

No. She was real, all right. As real as a heartbeat. A little older but even more beautiful than he remembered—which, until this moment, he would've deemed an impossibility. He knew she was from Williamson, but he'd never imagined he'd find her here like this.

Not now. Not today.

"Deputy Cole, I'm Sheriff Mercer."

Harlan blinked, then swiveled his head to his left to find a sunbaked cowboy in a gray suit with a string tie rising from his chair, his hand extended.

Harlan reached out and shook it, happy for the distraction. "Good to meet you, Sheriff. I wish it were under better circumstances."

"You sure you're up to this? Looks like your boy did quite a job on you."

Harlan had hoped that the bruise wouldn't be that noticeable—a symbol of his failure— but it didn't much matter. He'd just have to learn to live with it for the next several days.

"I'll be fine, thanks. But if you don't mind, I think I'll sit down."

Mercer gestured to a chair. "By all means."

Harlan glanced at Callie, then pulled the chair out, as Mercer introduced the people around the table. The names and faces came at him too quickly to process, but when the sheriff got to the only one Harlan really cared about, she finally looked up at him, offering him a curt, professional smile.

Her *eyes* weren't smiling, however. Not even close. And her voice had a clipped, unfriendly tone. "Hello, Harlan."

He nodded. "Callie."

Mercer's eyebrows went up. "You two know each other?"

"Long time ago," she said. "Back in graduate school. We took a couple of criminology classes together."

She'd said this with about as much warmth and enthusiasm as an accountant reciting the tax code. There was a lot more to it than that, but she wasn't offering any details. Which was fine by Harlan. He didn't want to *think* about those details—although he was finding it difficult not to.

Mercer said, "Denver, right? University of Colorado?"

"Right," they said in unison.

They exchanged an awkward glance as Mercer studied them curiously, then sat back down.

"Small world," he said, "but I reckon you two can catch up some other time. Right now we've got business to attend to." He looked at Harlan. "Your supervising deputy says you've got some information to share."

Harlan tore his gaze away from Callie and nodded. He had spent the better part of his morning at the Torrington marshal's substation gathering up as much intel on Billy Boy Lyman as he could find. He hadn't had much sleep since the incident, and his supervisor back in Colorado Springs had urged him to take it easy and let someone else handle the heavy lifting.

But Harlan had refused.

He preferred to clean up his own messes.

When he'd heard that his Glock had been found under a burned-out pickup truck near Williamson—a vehicle carrying the body of a local rancher—he'd made a vow right then and there that he wouldn't rest until Billy Boy was back in custody.

Or begging St. Peter to open up the pearly gates.

"First," he said, "I want to apologize to all of you for making any of this necessary. If I hadn't been derelict in my duties, none of us would be sitting here right now."

He glanced at Callie again but got nothing back. She was carefully examining her fingernails.

"Let's not worry about blame," Mercer said. "The way I look at it, the only reason we're here is because of this boy Lyman."

"Thanks, Sheriff, I appreciate that." Harlan reached into his coat pocket and brought out a small stack of photographs. "I assume you all saw the mug shot I faxed over?"

There were nods and murmurs around the room.

"Lyman's a Nebraska native who moved with his mother to Wyoming when he was sixteen years old. He's been in and out of custody ever since, his latest bust for an aborted robbery attempt at the Colorado Springs Bank and Trust three weeks ago. He was out on parole at the time, and since the courts are backed up, someone on high figured it wouldn't hurt to ship his butt up to Torrington to finish out his state sentence while he's waiting for trial. That's where I came in."

He laid the stack of photos on the table. "We took these from the convenience store's surveillance footage. The main unit was destroyed, but the owner keeps a backup in his office closet."

"How's the clerk doing?"

The question came from a young guy sitting next to Callie. Rusty-something.

"Touch and go, last I heard."

Harlan had found the clerk tied up and shoved into a storeroom, his head caved in by a blow much harder than the one he himself had received. Once he saw the poor guy, he knew that he could easily have wound up in the very same condition. So maybe getting beaned by Billy Boy instead of the girlfriend or the potato chip lover was a blessing he should be thankful for.

Tapping the photos, he said, "These are the two perpetrators who helped Lyman escape. We think they may have been his partners in the bank job, but they were wearing ski masks at the time and managed to get away."

Mercer said, "You run those photos through facial recognition?"

Harlan nodded. "No hits so far, which isn't

much of a surprise considering how bad the resolution is." He looked at the others. "We found their Chevy Malibu dumped in a field about sixty miles north of the convenience store. Broken water pump. That's probably where they hitched a ride with the victim. And since people tend to go where they feel most comfortable, I'm hoping they might be local. Maybe one of you crossed paths with them at one time or another."

He slid the photos to Mercer, who picked up the stack and started shuffling through it. Within seconds, something shifted in the sheriff's eyes. "Well I'll be damned. This is getting cozier and cozier."

"You recognize them?"

Mercer didn't answer. Instead he took a photo off the top of the stack and spun it across the table toward Callie. "That face look familiar to you?"

Callie caught it, then dropped her gaze, studying the image carefully.

After a moment, she said, "Looks like Megan Pritchard, but this is a little fuzzy and it's been a while. She hasn't been around much since her last stint in juvie, and that was like—what?—three, four years ago?"

Mercer shrugged. "Give or take."

"So who is she?" Harlan asked.

"Megan Pritchard-Breen," Callie said. "Only nobody uses the Breen part since her mother got a divorce years ago. She's one of our local troublemakers. Sheriff here likes to call her a wild child, but I think he's being polite in deference to the family. Sociopath is more accurate."

"She's also a bit of a fire bug," Mercer told him. "So draw your own conclusions."

"And she's got family up here?"

Mercer glanced at Callie, and Harlan followed his lead, but she once again averted her gaze. He sensed, however, that this time it had nothing to do with their past. There was a different kind of history at play here. An underlying discomfort she wasn't anxious to address. And Harlan had the feeling he was the only one in the room who didn't know about it.

"She's the granddaughter of Jonah Pritchard," Mercer said. "And if you spent any significant amount of time in Williamson, you'd recognize the name."

"Local celebrity?"

"That's one way of putting it, if you like 'em old and mean and wealthier than the crown prince of Tangiers."

"I take it you're not a fan."

"Let's just say the pathology seems to run in the family, only Jonah is a little better at hiding it." He looked at Callie. "And if that *is* Megan Pritchard, I think you know what it means."

She frowned. "You want Rusty and me to go out there."

"I know you've got issues with the old coot, but you *are* the lead deputy on this case."

"Out where?" Harlan asked.

"Pritchard Ranch," Mercer said. "If Meg's in trouble, she'd go to her grandpa for help. Always has, always will."

"Which means Billy Boy might be there, as well."

"That's the logical assumption. So I'd suggest you three saddle up, pronto. We don't have a warrant, but maybe the Pritchards will cooperate."

Harlan nodded, then got to his feet.

"Wait a minute," Callie said, her frown deepening. "You want him to go *with* us?"

Mercer's brows went up again. "Is that a problem? I thought you two were old friends."

Harlan and Callie exchanged another glance, neither of them willing to tackle that one in public, and Harlan could feel the eyes of everyone in the room shifting in his direction. The office gossip line would be buzzing this afternoon.

Mercer tapped his watch. "Tick tock, Deputy Glass. We've got a trio of killers to catch."

Looking like a woman who had just been condemned to a decade of indentured servitude, Callie reluctantly rolled her chair back and stood up.

Harlan knew exactly how she felt.

Chapter Four

"How much farther is it?" Harlan asked.

These were more or less the first words spoken since the three of them had climbed into Callie's cruiser. Now that Harlan had broken the silence, Rusty—who had probably sensed the tension in the air and had been smart enough to keep his mouth shut—gestured from the front passenger seat, saying, "Just up the road apiece. About five or six miles."

To Callie's mind, it might as well be five or six *hundred*. With all due respect to the late Jim Farber and his family, she couldn't wait until this day was over. From Nana Jean's matchmaking to the surprise appearance of a man she loathed and now this trip out to Pritchard Ranch—the *last* place she wanted to go—this was turning out to be a record breaker. All future days would surely be measured against this one.

Callie had never considered herself a vindictive woman. She'd never been one to hold on to a grudge. More often than not she found she could remain civil with the tiny handful of men she'd been intimate with. She had long ago convinced herself that she was a much better friend than lover.

But the breakup with Harlan had been different. Maybe it was her immaturity, or maybe it was the simple fact that she had been so head over heels in love with him. Whatever the cause, she had carried this burning resentment toward him a lot longer than she wanted to admit.

It rarely came to the surface, however. No reason it should. She hadn't seen Harlan in nearly a decade, and had long since learned to get through a day, a week, sometimes even a whole month, without thinking about him. But every time she *did*, she found herself hating him all over again.

She knew, of course, that her anger was simply a way of masking the pain. Not just because of the breakup, but because of the circumstances surrounding it.

She'd bet good money that if the accident hadn't happened, she and Harlan would still be together. No question. But that tragic night had forced such an enormous wedge between them that it was no wonder they could barely stand to look at each other.

Callie didn't think she would ever forgive Harlan for what he'd done. And until today it hadn't been much of an issue.

Now here he was, sitting in the backseat of her SUV, and it took every bit of inner strength she could muster to keep from slamming the brakes and throwing him out in the middle of the highway.

The thing that *really* galled her, however, was that despite her turmoil she couldn't stop thinking about how good he looked. The years had given his face and body an angularity, a solid, rustic dignity that had only been hinted at in his younger days. He'd been attractive back then, no doubt about it, but now he looked as if he'd just stepped out of a movie screen, his blue-eyed Hollywood good looks tempered with just enough real-world ruggedness to make him a genuine human being.

And that was all the more reason to hate him. He should be suffering for what he'd done. Balding and getting too fat and covered in festering boils.

Tell us how you really feel, Callie.

Gripping the wheel tighter, she punched the accelerator and picked up speed.

THE PRITCHARD FAMILY had always displayed their wealth without apology. Nestled in the foothills of the Bighorn Mountains, the ranch was seven thousand acres of rolling hills, grassy flatland and a sleekly modern, three-story dream house that was big enough to hold the population of a small third-world country.

As she pulled up to the gate, Callie thought about her connection to the family. Despite the shared blood, she had long ago realized that there really *wasn't* one. Not the kind that mattered, at least. Before she was even born, Jonah Pritchard had made it clear that neither she nor her mother were worth spitting on, and Callie herself couldn't care less about his money.

Everyone in town knew the history between the two families. A few of her friends—including Sheriff Mercer—had urged her to pursue her stake in the Pritchard fortune. When her father was killed, he'd left behind a sizable trust that rightfully belonged to her. But pursuing it meant lawsuits and court hearings and exhumed bodies and DNA tests and a lot of bad feelings all around.

If Callie went forward, she knew full well that Jonah would wage a smear campaign against the memory of her mother. He'd hire a platoon of lawyers and PR flacks to claim the DNA tests had somehow been tainted or tampered with, claiming the girl had slept around like a common whore and that Callie could be just about *anyone's* child.

There was no amount of money that would dull the sting of such an attack, especially in a town the size of Williamson, which had less than seven thousand residents—the majority of whom loved to gossip. And with Nana Jean getting frailer by the week, it just wasn't worth it.

Callie was content to know that she had *earned* her place in this world. And she couldn't help thinking how ironic it was that Megan, the so-called *real* Pritchard granddaughter, had turned out to be a family embarrassment. No smear campaign necessary.

Callie had to admit she'd found a certain satisfaction in this knowledge.

As she pulled her cruiser to a stop, the guard manning the gate came out of his booth and approached her window with a smile on his face. Landry Bickham was a grizzled old cowboy who had been working for the Pritchard family as long as anyone could remember, and Callie didn't think she'd ever seen him without that smile.

"Afternoon, Deputy Glass. You sure you didn't make a wrong turn?"

"If only," she said. "I need to go up to the house. Police business."

Bickham grunted. "You make an appointment?"

Callie just stared at him.

Bickham nodded, then went back to the booth and picked up the phone. Callie knew she could ask him if he'd seen Megan in the past few hours, but there wasn't much point. Landry was loyal to a fault—the secret behind his longevity on the job.

After his call was done, he came back shaking his head, the smile still intact. "Jonah is a little under the weather today, isn't taking any visitors."

"I already told you, this isn't a social call."

Bickham shrugged. "You might try again tomorrow morning."

"Open the gate, Landry."

"I really wish I could do that, Callie, but I've got my—"

Before Landry could finish his sentence, Harlan had his door open and was climbing out. He brushed the flap of his coat back, revealing the star clipped to his belt. "U.S. Marshals Service. Open that gate now or consider yourself under arrest."

Bickham's smile faltered slightly. "For what?"

"For aiding and abetting a fugitive. Or for being a general pain in the butt. Take your choice."

Callie couldn't help feeling a little annoyed by Harlan's intrusion. Didn't he think she could get the job done?

Apparently not.

"Fugitive? What fugitive?" Bickham said. "I'm just following orders."

Callie gestured impatiently. "Do what he asks, Landry. I'll make sure Jonah knows you put up a good fight."

"Is this fella really gonna arrest me?"

"Not if you cooperate."

"All right, then," Bickham said, then shuffled back to his booth and flipped a switch. The gate rumbled and started rolling to one side.

As Harlan got back in the car, Callie hit

the gas, shooting forward before he had a chance to sit down and get his door closed.

He yelped, letting loose a string of profanities, and she eyed him in her rearview mirror.

"You okay back there?"

Struggling to collect himself, Harlan shot her a look of annoyance that kept her smiling all the way up the drive.

No, she wasn't vindictive.

Not one little bit.

Chapter Five

Landry Bickham hadn't wasted any time in sounding the alarm.

They were greeted at the top of the drive by Gloria Pritchard, a woman whose beauty had been starkly diminished by years of starvation, alcohol and cosmetic surgery. The result was the exact opposite of what she had intended, her skin stretched so tautly over her sharp bones that she looked much older than her fifty-one years.

Callie only knew her actual age because Gloria and her mother had been best friends in high school. Not that this mattered much. Gloria visibly stiffened at the sight of Callie as they climbed out of the SUV.

Neither of them offered any pleasantries.

"So what has my little darling done *now?*" Gloria asked. The *little darling* being her wayward daughter Meg.

"Is she here?"

"I haven't seen her in a good six months."

"Then what makes you think that's what this is about?"

Gloria smiled humorlessly. "Experience," she said. "I don't need to tell you what a handful that girl has been since the day she was born."

To put it mildly, Callie thought. Megan Pritchard was the devil incarnate as far as she was concerned. But without the brains. Even her own mother had stopped trying to cover for her.

Not that Gloria was the model of a loving parent. Twice divorced and always shopping for a replacement, she paid about as much attention to her own daughter as she might a pet hamster.

Meg's grandfather Jonah, on the other hand, would do just about anything for his girl—whether Gloria liked it or not.

"What about your father?"

Gloria seemed to grow even more tense. "What about him?"

"Has *he* seen her? Recently, I mean. Like the last twelve or so hours."

"I'm afraid I wouldn't know," she said.

"This is a big house, and Jonah and I tend to avoid each other as much as possible."

One thing you could say about Gloria was that, despite her family's money and the Hollywood housewife exterior, she was always brutally frank and open about her feelings, even when it meant exposing the truth about their not-so-happy family.

Maybe it was the years of AA meetings.

"You still haven't answered my question," she said. "What's Meg done now?"

Harlan apparently took this as his cue to step forward, reaching into his inner coat pocket as he did.

"Ma'am, I'm Deputy U.S. Marshal Harlan Cole. I'd like you to take a look at this, if you don't mind."

He brought out one of the surveillance photographs and handed it to her.

"Is this your daughter?"

Gloria took a long moment to study the image, then said, "I think so, yes."

Harlan nodded. "You say you haven't seen her in six months, but when's the last time you spoke to her?"

Gloria returned the photograph. "She called me a few days ago. Just to remind me how much she despises me."

"She happen to mention she was headed your way?"

"No," Gloria said.

"Well, we have reason to believe she was, and after last night, she's in the company of at least one wanted fugitive and may well have participated in a bank robbery and a murder." He paused, glancing at Callie as if seeking some kind of approval. She wasn't sure why. He seemed content with running the show. "In light of this," he said to Gloria, "I'd like your permission to search the premises."

Before Gloria could answer, a stern baritone boomed. "I'm afraid you're out of luck, Marshal."

They all turned to find Jonah Pritchard standing in the doorway, a tall man in blue jeans and a dark flannel shirt. He was close to Nana Jean's age, but with none of the frailty. In fact, he was as solid as a twenty-year-old and didn't look even remotely under the weather.

Callie knew she should probably feel something. After all, he was *her* grandfather, too. But feelings are reserved for those you care about, and she'd have to reach down pretty deep to find anything that resembled an emotional attachment to this man.

"*I* own this house," he said to Harlan, "and permission is definitely not granted."

Harlan stepped toward him now, once again flashing the badge on his hip. "Then I guess you'd be Jonah Pritchard."

"That's right," the old man said.

"Well, I was only asking to be polite, sir, so if you'll move to one side, we'd like to get started."

Callie threw him a look.

Say *what?*

Jonah shook his head. "Without a warrant? If you want to come in, you'll need a judge's signature."

Harlan cocked a brow at him, then turned to Callie and Rusty. "Did you two hear that?"

Callie frowned, not sure what he was getting at. "What?"

"He just asked me if I want to come in. Sounded like an invitation to me."

Uh-oh, Callie thought. So Harlan was one of those. She was a strong believer in procedure and didn't appreciate the cowboys who ignored it in hopes of getting a pass from the courts. She should've realized he was a

"Wyatt Earp" the minute he jumped out of her SUV to confront Landry.

But before she could tell him that neither she nor Rusty were about to play along, Jonah stepped aside, moving out onto the wide front porch. Not to invite them in, but to make room for a couple of burly ranch hands who emerged from the doorway behind him.

He looked pointedly at Harlan. "You take one more step in this direction, I'm within my rights to stop you."

Callie watched as Harlan studied the two ranch hands. They weren't carrying weapons, but then they didn't need to.

Harlan said, "Not like this, you aren't. The law doesn't look too kindly on assault against peace officers."

Jonah shrugged. "It isn't too thrilled about illegal search and seizure, either. And it won't keep these boys from putting you three in the hospital." He gestured to his daughter. "Gloria, get in the house. No reason for you to be here for this."

In other words, *get lost*.

Callie could see the resentment in Gloria's eyes. Resentment that went back many years.

But Gloria did as she was told. And without protest.

When she was gone, Jonah said, "There's no need for this to get ugly, Marshal."

Now Callie spoke up. "Tell that to Megan, Mr. Pritchard. And to Jim Farber's family. She and her friends left him in quite a state."

"I wouldn't know anything about that."

"Wouldn't you?"

He gave her a look that said he was offended by the remark, but she sensed he was feigning it. Nothing she said could offend him. The old guy was bulletproof.

"Meg decided a long time ago that she wasn't interested in associating with this family," he said. "Not that that's any of your business."

Callie knew that his words were meant to cut much deeper than they did, but after thirty-four years she was immune to him. She'd long been aware that Jonah despised her. By his skewed logic, his son wouldn't be dead if it weren't for her whore of a mother.

The thought of this suddenly brought to surface another part of her life—her years with Harlan—and she wondered for a brief moment if she'd applied her own skewed logic to that situation.

But no. That was different. And she had no desire to wander into any dark alleys right now.

Focus, Callie.

Concentrate on the matter at hand.

"We could clear all this up," Harlan said to Jonah, "if you'd just let us do our job. If you've got nothing to hide, then this conversation is over."

"It's already over," a voice said, and Callie heard the ratchet of a scatter-gun behind them.

She and Harlan and Rusty all turned to find a smiling Landry Bickham holding a pump-action twelve-gauge. He kept it pointed at the ground, but Callie knew he'd use it if the old man gave him the nod.

Her heart started thumping.

This wasn't the direction she'd wanted this afternoon to go.

Harlan turned back to Jonah. "You're making a grave mistake, Mr. Pritchard. I could arrest you for obstruction, right now."

"I suppose you could try," Jonah said.

They were all silent for a long moment, and Callie could see the fury creeping into

Harlan's gaze. She'd seen that fury before, when she told him she never wanted to lay eyes on him again.

Jonah gestured. "You go on, now, try to get your warrant. If the judge says I've gotta open up my house, I'll open up my house. In the meantime, you're just trespassing, far as I can see."

For a moment Callie thought Harlan might do something stupid, but he held back. Thank God.

"This isn't over," he said quietly.

Jonah's gaze didn't waver. "I don't doubt that for a minute."

Harlan stared at him a while longer, then his fury seemed to dissipate and he turned, moving back to the cruiser.

Then they were all inside, Callie feeling both frustrated and relieved as she started the engine and watched Jonah and the others go back into the house.

"You think they're in there?" Harlan asked.

Callie wanted to punch him. "Even if they are, unless Pritchard cooperates, there's not much we can do about it right now."

"He's one nasty piece of work, isn't he?"

Callie jammed the car in gear. "Pot…meet kettle," she said.

Then she turned them around and headed down the drive.

Chapter Six

"You know what you are? You're an idiot. An idiot disguised as a fool."

Good old Callie. She'd never been one to mince words, and Harlan could see that she hadn't changed.

Back in the day it had been a trait he'd found endearing. Most of the girls he'd known in college had been hesitant to show their true colors until they had you on the hook. They spent far too much time playing the games they'd learned in high school, and the guys they pursued weren't much different.

But Callie had always been what-you-see-is-what-you-get. Take it or leave it. And that was a large part of what had made Harlan fall in love with her in the first place.

That and the simple fact that she was the

single most intriguing human being he'd ever met. Still was.

They were rolling along the highway now, headed toward town, Harlan once again relegated to the backseat while Callie drove and her partner Rusty rode shotgun.

She said, "You do realize you almost got us killed back there."

Harlan looked at her reflection in the rearview mirror. "Don't be so dramatic. Pritchard doesn't strike me as stupid. And technically, he was right."

"You *think?*" Her hands were gripping the steering wheel as if she had hold of his neck and wanted to snap it. "Then what was with all that cowboy nonsense?"

"Just giving the old guy a nudge, see how he reacted."

Callie shook her head. "You haven't changed at all, have you, Harlan?"

"I beg your pardon?"

"Forget it," she muttered.

"No, you opened the box, let's see what's inside."

Callie sighed, glancing at Rusty. He had his cell phone clamped to his ear, speaking quietly into it, pretending not to listen to them.

She said to Harlan, "Maybe Jonah wouldn't have done anything drastic, but there were no guarantees of that. You make stupid moves, you risk people getting hurt. You should know that better than anyone."

Harlan knew a lot of things. Like the fact that she wasn't talking about Pritchard at all.

"Look," he said, "why don't we save the recriminations for another day? Right now we need to concentrate on searching that house. And we need to do it legally."

"That could be a problem," Rusty said, snapping his phone shut. "Sheriff Mercer tells me the judge went out of town for a weekend hunting trip. He's trying to track down another judge in Sheridan, but it could take a while. Says we might as well grab some chow, then head back to the station house."

Now it was Harlan's turn to sigh. Times like these made him wish real life was more like the movies. Everything happened so quickly on the big screen. Getting a warrant took minutes rather than hours, and the bad guy rarely got away.

He kept thinking about that smirk on Billy Boy's face, and would like to put a fist in it. But as much as he'd like to play the hero and storm Pritchard Ranch, he believed in the letter of the law and knew that such a move was a mistake for a whole variety of reasons.

One thing you quickly learned in law enforcement was the value of patience. No matter what they might say, Justice was neither swift nor blind.

"Maybe the sheriff is right," he said. "I haven't had a bite to eat since yesterday afternoon. By all rights I should be famished."

Callie eyed him skeptically. "You really expect me to sit down and break bread with you?"

"I expect you to be a professional," he told her. "Is that too much to ask?"

EVERY TOWN HAS ITS cop hangout.

Williamson's was a place called the Oak Pit Bar & Grill, a name Callie had always found a bit odd, since Wyoming wasn't known for its overabundance of *Quercus imbricaria.* But she supposed the Cottonwood Pit didn't have the same ring.

As far as she knew, however, there were no trees in evidence here, the indoor barbecue fueled by coals rather than wood. The low lighting and pool hall atmosphere were not to her particular taste, but she couldn't argue with the food they served, and cops all over Williamson County had made the place a regular pit stop.

No pun intended.

Callie didn't want to be sitting in a booth across from Harlan Cole, but she knew he was right. As cruel as fate might be, she was a professional and needed to act like one.

Truth was, she was more concerned about Rusty than herself. Poor guy was caught in the middle of a rich and heated history that he knew nothing about. And as his training deputy, she owed it to him to maintain her composure.

Besides, she was hungry. Thanks to Nana Jean's torturous attempt at matchmaking this afternoon, she hadn't had a chance to eat before she'd been called back to the office.

So here they were, the three of them sitting there awkwardly as they waited on their food, poor Rusty trying to make small talk with two people who clearly had other matters on their minds.

"How long you been with the Marshals Service?" he asked Harlan.

Harlan pulled his gaze away from the sports report on a nearby flatscreen. "Close to ten years."

"You trained at Glynco, right? Out in Georgia?"

"That's right."

Rusty leaned back, took a sip of the ice tea he'd ordered. "I did my basic at the Wyoming Law Enforcement Academy in Douglas, but for a while there I had my eye on Glynco and the Marshals Service. Recruiter approached me while I was still in college." He looked at Callie. "Same with you, right? You almost went federal."

Callie stiffened slightly. "Yes."

"So what changed your mind?"

"Circumstances," she said tersely, but didn't feel like elaborating. Those circumstances were sitting across the table from her.

Rusty gave her room to continue, but when he realized she was finished, he said to Harlan, "So anyway, I decided I'd rather stay local. No chance of being transferred across country, and I like Wyoming. Good place to raise a family. You got family?"

"Brother in California. That's about it."

"Have you always been in Colorado Springs, or do they move you around a lot?"

"I've bounced around a little, but Colorado seems to be the best fit. Been there five years."

"They keep you busy, I guess. Transporting prisoners—that must be pretty interesting sometimes."

"It has its moments," Harlan said. "Especially when one of them smacks you in the head with your own weapon."

Rusty smiled. "At least you've got a sense of humor about it."

"One of my trainers at Glynco always said, you don't find a reason to laugh, you might as well hang it up."

"Amen," Rusty murmured.

Callie was thinking that *she* could use a reason to laugh right now, when someone called out to Rusty—one of the fake-boobed, underdressed cop groupies who rolled in every evening looking for attention. She was standing near an available pool table, gesturing to him with the cue stick in her hand.

Rusty gave her a wave, then turned to Callie. "Citizen needs assistance," he said. "Call me when the food comes."

Callie rolled her eyes. She could just imagine the kind of assistance the girl needed, but this was Rusty's chance to escape the torture and she couldn't blame him. He quickly slipped out of the booth and left them alone.

Harlan watched him go. "I used to be that young once."

Callie scoffed. "You're what—thirty-five? Not exactly Jonah Pritchard territory."

"It'll happen soon enough. Goes by fast, doesn't it? The past ten years are barely a blip on the radar."

Callie had to admit he was right. She sometimes felt as if she had stepped onto a bullet train, the past decade an indistinct blur of joys and heartbreaks and not much in between.

She found herself thinking about the heartbreak that had torn them apart, when Harlan glanced at her left hand and asked, "You never got married?"

She stiffened again. Why was he asking her that? What difference did it make?

"Cops and marriage don't mix," she said.

He nodded. "I found that out the hard way."

She felt a small stab of disappointment. She shouldn't have cared, but for some reason she did. "You were married?"

"Thirteen months," he said. "Lucky number."

"When was this?"

"About a year after you and I split. But I don't know what I was thinking. I knew it was a mistake before it even happened."

"Why?"

His gaze locked on hers, those blue eyes enough to make any woman's legs tremble. Even one who hated his guts.

"Because she wasn't you," he said.

HE DIDN'T KNOW WHY he'd said it.

The words came out impulsively, a surprise even to him. He could just as easily have told her that he and his ex simply hadn't been in love. But he didn't often think about his marriage, and until this moment he'd never realized that *Callie* was the reason it had been doomed from the start.

Because she wasn't you.

The minute he said it he was plagued by regret, inwardly cursing himself for being so impulsive. He knew how Callie felt about him and she wasn't likely to be receptive to such a statement.

It was no real shock when she sat up slightly, looking as if he'd slapped her across the face.

"What did you just say?"

"Forget it," he told her. "That just slipped out. Don't pay any attention to—"

"You say something like that and you think I'm suddenly going to fall all over you? 'Oh, Harlan, it's so good to see you after all these years. Oh, Harlan, I never should've—'"

"Stop," he said. "This isn't funny."

Callie paused, studying him soberly. "What you did hurt me, Harlan."

"I didn't *do* anything."

"Didn't you? These past ten years may have gone by fast, but they don't change the fact that you're the reason Treacher is dead."

So there it was. The thing that had been simmering between them ever since he'd walked into that conference room. They'd both known it was there, but neither of them had been willing to say it out loud. Until now.

She still blamed him for the accident.

He and Treacher and Callie had been inseparable in college. The *Three Amigos*, everyone called them—a study group that had morphed into a solid, unwavering friendship. And for Harlan and Callie, it became something much deeper.

Treacher had been their best friend, like a

brother to both of them, and to say his death was devastating was to understate its impact a thousandfold.

And while Harlan had suspected Callie still blamed him, hearing her express this sentiment with such unflagging conviction— just as she had on their last night together— gave him every reason to get up and walk out of this place without another word.

Instead he said, "I'm not asking for anything from you, Callie. I'm here to catch a wanted man. That's all. And if you have problems with me, I'd just as soon you keep them to yourself." He got to his feet. "Now, if you don't mind, I think I'll get my order to go."

He started to walk away, but thought better of it and stopped, turning back to look at her.

"Just so you know, the reason I said what I said about my marriage is because it's true. I was in love with you, even after you made it clear you wanted nothing to do with me. And every woman I met after we broke up was measured against you. Against what we had before Treacher was killed." He paused. "You may think you have every right to feel the way you feel, but I'm *not* the reason he's dead. If you want to attribute blame, then why not look at the real culprit? Treacher himself."

He expected her say something, but she remained silent. Wouldn't look at him now. And he knew that what he'd just told her hadn't penetrated. The barrier she'd erected was too high and wide and thick, and trying to get through it was impossible.

So why even bother?

Turning, he flagged the waitress and headed across the bar to get his food.

Chapter Seven

She was staring at her half-eaten burger when the call came.

After returning to the table, Rusty had given up on her and had taken his food across the bar to sit with the girl with the fake boobs.

Callie hadn't put up much of a protest. She'd wanted to be alone. To think about Harlan and what he'd said.

Because she wasn't you.

There was so much heartbreak in those words that she'd found it nearly impossible to maintain her composure.

How do you react when someone tells you something like that? Someone you once loved so deeply you thought life simply couldn't go on without him?

Do you let go of all the animosity you've nurtured? Do you set aside the pain—the pain he still refused to take responsibility for?

Apparently not, if your name is Callie Glass. And not because you don't *want* to but because you *can't*.

Callie had tried many times over the years, had even thought about getting in touch with Harlan, had often wondered where life had taken him.

But she'd always held back.

Always.

The sting of Treacher's death had ruptured something inside her. A vital organ had been damaged and refused to heal. And every time she picked up the phone, or thought about entering the name *Harlan Cole* into a search engine, she had stopped herself.

She would remember all those crazy late nights when the three of them would get drunk together and talk about the future. Their plans to join the Marshals Service, to request assignments in the same jurisdiction, to raise families in the same neighborhood and have backyard barbecues and birthday parties and cheer their kids on at soccer games.

In short, they were inseparable.

The *Three Amigos*.

And beneath it all was the assumption that Callie and Harlan would get married.

Treacher would often smile that crooked smile of his and say, "The two of you were born to be together. God pointed you on a path toward each other from the moment you were conceived."

What they were all witnessing, he told them, was destiny in motion.

A plan perfectly executed.

On hearing this Harlan would pull Callie into his lap and put his arms around her as she leaned back against him, languishing in the heat of his embrace.

"Soul mates," he'd say softly, the warmth of his breath against her ear. And later when Treacher had gone home, they would lie together on Harlan's bed, making love with an urgent passion that Callie had never since felt.

They both knew that Treacher was right. The bond between them—between all of them—was shatterproof.

Or so they had thought.

They couldn't know that God apparently had different plans. That Treacher would be dead within months, taking that crooked smile and their relationship along with him. That the man who was so convinced that they were meant to be together would become the reason they broke apart.

And when Callie remembered this, she would hang up the phone or close down the search engine and try not to cry.

She didn't *want* to hate Harlan. She just couldn't help herself. Maybe because that hate was the one true thing in her life these days. The one true thing that made her feel alive. Or maybe it was the thing that helped assuage her *own* guilt for not being there that night. For choosing to forego the party because finals were approaching and she felt so desperately behind. After all, if she failed any of her courses she wouldn't get her degree in criminology, and that would screw up the timeline they'd all mapped out.

The irony in this wasn't lost on her. Maybe if she'd taken a short break, just an hour or two away from the books, she could have done what Harlan had failed to do and everything would be on track.

Treacher would be alive.

And she and Harlan would be…

Way to wallow in the mud, Callie.

She shook her head and stared morosely at her half-eaten burger, chastising herself for getting caught up in this nonsense again. She had a *new* life now. A job she did well in a town where she felt wanted. Friends, people who loved her. Nana Jean.

She needed to suck it up and get past this day. Bury her feelings for a while and do what the county of Williamson paid her to do. Help Harlan catch his fugitive and Jim Farber's killer, then say goodbye to the past once and for all.

She had convinced herself that this was exactly what she was going to do, when her cell phone bleeped and she put it to her ear.

"Deputy Glass."

"Callie?"

The voice was familiar. "Yes, who is this?"

"It's Judith, dear. Judith Patterson. I don't want you to worry, but we're on our way to County Memorial and I think you need to meet us there."

"What's wrong?" Callie asked. "What happened?"

"It's your Nana Jean," Judith told her. "She's had an accident."

CALLIE GOT TO THE HOSPITAL shortly after Judith and Nana Jean arrived. Judith was guiding Nana through the Emergency Room doorway, Nana keeping a towel clamped to her forehead.

"I'm all right," she said, "it's just a cut. No big deal."

Callie took over for Judith. "What happened?"

"I tripped on that stupid throw rug. Hit my head on the edge of the coffee table. I don't know why Judith insisted I come here."

But when Callie caught Judith's gaze, she could see from her look that there was more to it than that.

A few minutes later a nurse brought a wheelchair and rolled Nana into the exam room and Judith turned to Callie.

"I saw the whole thing," she said. "She didn't trip. She had one of her dizzy spells and fell."

Callie nodded. "That's what I was afraid of."

"There was a lot of blood, too. Thank God Henry and I were there to drive her to the hospital."

Callie glanced out the large bay windows toward the parking lot and saw the plumber lock his van before heading toward the Emergency Room.

Had Nana invited Judith and him back to the house for dinner?

Did she not listen to Callie at *all?*

"It's getting to the point where I don't feel comfortable leaving her alone," she said to Judith. "I'm gonna have to find some kind of solution. Hire a caregiver or something."

"Well, don't say that too loud. You're grandmother's as stubborn as they come and she won't take kindly to some stranger in the house."

Henry the plumber was getting closer by the moment. Callie had no idea if he was in on this matchmaking scheme, but she wasn't interested in yet another awkward moment. She'd had enough of those for one day.

"Well, she'll just have to get used to it," she told Judith, then started in the direction the nurse had wheeled Nana. "I'd better go check on her."

A moment later Callie was standing in a curtained cubicle as the doctor examined the gash on Nana's forehead.

"We'll put a butterfly bandage on it, but you won't need any stitches."

"I *told* Judith it was a just a scratch."

The doctor opened a drawer in a nearby cart. "Well, it's a bit more than that Ms.

Glass. She was smart to bring you here. Head wounds tend to bleed a lot and you could have lost a significant amount of blood."

Nana frowned. "Oh, for goodness sake, you'd think it was the first time I ever cut myself."

"Judith had a right to be concerned," Callie said. "Did you tell the doctor about the dizzy spell?"

The doctor's eyebrows went up. "Dizzy spell?"

Nana looked at Callie as if she'd just betrayed a sacred trust. "I see Judith has been flapping her mouth again. So what if I get dizzy once in a while—what's the big deal?"

The doctor took a cotton swab from the drawer. "Dizzy spells are not the kind of thing you want to ignore, Ms. Glass. Especially a woman your age."

"What are you talking about? I'm only seventy-six. It's not like I'm on my deathbed."

"And some of us would like to keep it that way," Callie said.

The doctor nodded. "I think we should check you in for the night and run some tests. Try to find out why you're losing your balance."

"I'm perfectly fine," Nana said.

"This cut on your forehead says different. And I'd just as soon rule out anything serious before I release you."

Nana shot Callie another glance. "See what you've done?"

"Knock it off, Nana. It's for your own good."

The old woman sighed. "I don't see why you feel the need to try to run my life."

Callie couldn't help but smile. "Now you know how it feels."

It took them nearly an hour to get Nana Jean registered and into a room. By the time the nurse was done fussing with her, Nana had calmed down a bit, reluctantly coming to terms with the idea that she'd be spending the night.

"I hope you don't expect me to eat their food in the morning."

Callie was sitting in a chair next to the bed. "I'll bring you a treat," she said. "One of those cinnamon-raisin muffins from Bartly's Bakery."

Nana's eyes lit up. "Oooh, I do like those. That Edith Bartly knows her way around an oven."

"See? Being here's not so bad."

Nana scowled. "I still say it's a waste of—"

"*No,* Nana." Callie leaned forward and touched her wrist. "Anything that keeps you well is not a waste of time. If something were to happen to you, I don't know what I'd do with myself. You're the only real family I've got."

Callie suddenly felt tears in her eyes, but did her best to hold them back. To see the woman who raised her lying in a hospital bed with an oxygen tube in her nose got her thinking about just how tenuous life could be. She knew full well that, in a matter of seconds, someone you cared about—someone you loved—could go from a filling a hole in your heart to creating one.

She'd had enough of that in her life.

She knew she couldn't hang on to Nana forever, but she wasn't about to let the old woman slip away because of some stubborn, misplaced sense of pride. She could only hope that these dizzy spells were nothing serious.

Nana smiled. "Look at you, getting all misty-eyed. I don't think I've seen you cry since…" She paused. "Well, it's been a long time."

Callie wiped at her eyes. "Not crying," she said.

"It's all these nasty germs in the air, right?"

Now Callie smiled. "Right."

Nana was quiet for a moment, lost in a thought. Then she said, "I don't tell you this very often, Cal, but since the day you were born, you're the reason I breathe air every morning."

"Oh, Nana..."

"It was hard losing your mom—my sweet little Mary. Seeing the life go out of her eyes right there in front of me. But then I saw that light in you and I knew...I *knew* why I was put on this earth."

Callie gently squeezed her wrist. "Now you're *trying* to make me cry."

"Looks like it's working, too."

There was a sharp knock and Callie swiveled her head, surprised to find Rusty standing in the doorway.

"Sorry to interrupt," he said. "You feeling okay, Ms. Glass?"

"Just fine. Not that anyone's interested in listening to me."

"I'm sure the doctor knows what he's doing," Rusty told her, then shifted his gaze to Callie. "Tried calling you, but I guess they make you turn your phones off in here."

Callie quickly wiped at her eyes and nodded. "Did the judge sign the warrant?"

"Doesn't much matter at this point. We need to get moving."

"What's going on?" Callie asked, sensing his urgency.

"Just got a call from Deputy Cole. He's with Emergency Services. They're headed out to the Pritchard ranch."

"Why? What happened?"

"It's on fire," Rusty said.

Chapter Eight

The house was still ablaze when they got there.

The security gate was hanging open, two fire trucks out front, hoses blasting, water arcing toward the flames.

The sky was pitch-black now, the surrounding area illuminated only by the fire, and as Callie pulled her cruiser to a stop, a piercing scream rose from inside the house like something from another world.

Before she could even set the brake, she saw Harlan emerge from his own cruiser and start running. He pushed past the line of firefighters like a man possessed, and headed for the front door.

Callie's heart kicked up.

What on earth was he doing?

She watched in horror as a firefighter tried to grab hold of Harlan, but he spun and slipped away, then hurdled himself through the open doorway, ignoring the shouts of the men behind him, the house now looking as if it might collapse around him at any moment.

Oh, my God, she thought.

He's gone completely insane.

The screams rose again, a woman's voice begging—"Help me! Help me!"—and then Harlan disappeared entirely, swallowed by the fire.

Callie's heart thudded uncontrollably as she and Rusty jumped out of their cruiser and moved quickly to the line of firefighters.

"Why are you just standing here?" she shouted. "You have to go in after him!"

"Are you nuts?" one of the men said.

Then the biggest of them came over to her—an old friend from high school, Phil Dunworth. "That's a fool's errand, Callie. Wind blows the wrong direction, this place is coming down and I won't put my men at risk."

Stunned, Callie looked at the house as the flames continued to grow, her thudding heart threatening to burst through her chest. She couldn't quite believe that Harlan had gone inside there, but he'd once again proven that he was a cowboy and a reckless fool.

Before she realized it, her own feet were moving, heading in the direction of that door as Rusty shouted behind her—

"Callie! What are you doing? Stop!"

But she ignored him and pressed on, feeling a hot blast of air envelop her as she drew closer to the opening. She wasn't quite sure *why* she was doing this, but some buried instinct was tugging at her, forcing her to move.

Then suddenly Harlan emerged from the doorway, his arm around Gloria Pritchard's waist as she clung to him, desperately gasping for air. Her face was blank with shock and her right thigh was stained with blood, soaking through her jeans.

Callie rushed onto the porch and grabbed hold of Gloria, helping Harlan to keep her upright. Then several firefighters joined in, taking Gloria in their arms.

"I think she's been shot," Harlan said.

One of the men nodded as they whisked her toward a nearby ambulance. And as Callie and Harlan moved away from the house, Callie's heartbeat started to return to normal.

Harlan was out of breath, covered with soot and sweat, holding his left forearm in pain.

"You're an idiot," she said sourly.

"And you're in love with that word, aren't you?"

"It was stupid to go in there. You could've gotten yourself killed."

"Why do *you* care?"

She shot him a look. "Oh, come on, Harlan, that's not fair."

"I just did what had to be done," he said. "Now, if you don't mind, I've got some burns to attend to."

Then he picked up speed and continued across the yard to the ambulance.

LESS THAN AN HOUR LATER, all that was left of the Pritchard ranch house was a pile of charred rubble. A few hot spots still blazed, the fire boys doing their best to keep them down.

Callie stood with Rusty and Harlan, staring at the place in stunned disbelief.

"My God," she said.

The Pritchard ranch was an institution around here, a symbol of wealth and power. And despite what she might think of the Pritchards themselves, to see their home reduced to little more than black ash was both shocking and depressing. She'd never been one to find glee in other people's pain, even if she didn't much care for them.

Sheriff Mercer broke away from a group of firefighters and approached Callie and the others.

"Don't suppose it's much of a surprise," he told them, "but the arson boys are saying this wasn't an accident."

Harlan and Callie hadn't uttered more than a few syllables to each other since he'd emerged from the house with Gloria, and that was just fine with her. But now he said to Mercer, "Megan Pritchard, no doubt."

"Based on her history and the condition we found that pickup truck, I'd say that's a pretty good assumption."

"So we were right," Callie said. "Jonah was hiding her and her friends. Question is, where are they now? And where's Jonah?"

Mercer pointed to a spot near the center of the house, where a black lump could be seen, just barely, near a patch of flames that were struggling to stay alive.

Callie hadn't noticed it before. Another so-called crispy critter.

Oh, Lord.

She swallowed dryly.

"We're thinking he was probably shot,

too," Mercer said. "Won't know for sure until the medical examiner gets hold of him. Or what's left of him."

Harlan squinted at the body. "You sure that's Pritchard?"

"Got a witness says it is."

Callie was surprised. "Who?"

"Landry Bickham."

"Landry?" she said. She hadn't seen him in all the confusion. "Where is he?"

Mercer gestured to another ambulance across the tarmac. The first one had already taken Gloria to the hospital. "They found him in the backyard. I took a statement from him while Dudley Do-Right here was getting patched up."

The burns Harlan had suffered were minor, mostly to his hands and forearm. He ignored the jab and turned to Callie. "We're talking about the gatekeeper, right? The one with the shotgun?"

She nodded and Mercer said, "He's been with the Pritchards since high school. Says he tried to drag Gloria out of the back, but the smoke got to be too much for him."

"Is he conscious?" Harlan asked.

"They've got him on a gurney in there, but last I looked he was wide awake."

Harlan nodded and abruptly headed across the tarmac toward the ambulance.

Callie followed him.

The rear doors of the truck were hanging open to reveal Landry lying on the gurney inside, breathing through an oxygen mask as a paramedic tended to a burn on his forehead.

"Mr. Bickham?"

Landry rolled his eyes around in their sockets until his gaze was on Harlan. He reached up and pulled the mask aside, his trademark smile nowhere in evidence. "Still wanna arrest me?"

"Just need you to answer a few questions."

"I already told Sheriff Mercer what I know."

"I prefer to get my information firsthand," Harlan said.

"Can't stop you from asking."

"That's right. So why don't you tell me what happened here?"

"What do you think happened? House burnt down."

"I think there's more to it than that. Where were you when the fire started?"

Landry grabbed hold of the gurney rail and pulled himself upright. The paramedic tried to stop him, but Landry ignored the guy, keeping his gaze on Harlan. "You accusing me of something?"

"Are you *guilty* of something? I mean besides intimidating federal and county law enforcement deputies with a shotgun."

"I never pointed that weapon at you. And I was just doing what Jonah told me to."

"Did you always do what he told you to?"

"That *was* my job," Landry said.

"Did that include helping him hide his granddaughter and her two friends?"

Landry frowned. "What's Meg got to do with this?"

Callie moved up closer to the ambulance doors. "Come on, Landry, you know that's why we were here this afternoon."

"First I'm hearin' about it."

"Somehow I doubt that," Harlan said, "but let's get back to the fire. I'm gonna ask you again, where *were* you when it started?"

"Down at the south stable. Feeding the horses."

"What about the stable hands?" Callie asked.

"Jonah told me to send 'em home for the weekend. Along with the rest of the staff. I'm the only one stays on the premises 24/7."

"Why's that?"

Landry shrugged. "The Pritchards like their privacy. What difference does it make? It is what it is."

"How late does the staff usually stay?"

"Ranch hands do a six to three, house help seven to four, except for the cook, who preps dinner and is out by eight. But they were all gone by noon today, except for the boys you saw with Jonah. And they cut out right after you left."

"Why did he send everyone home so early?" Harlan asked.

"Hard as it may be to believe, Jonah Pritchard don't consult me on such matters. He said send 'em home, I sent 'em home."

It didn't take much to figure out why, Callie thought, but even if he knew, Landry would never tell. His loyalty went beyond the boundaries of death. Jonah may be gone, but he still had family with a reputation to uphold—as sketchy as it may already be— and Landry had been indoctrinated long ago.

Speak no evil.

"Okay," Harlan said. "So you were down at the south stable."

Landry nodded. "It's the one closest to the house—the Pritchards' private stock. Couple of the horses got skittish and I heard shouts, followed by some gunshots. So I figured I'd better get my butt up here. By the time I got to the house, the flames had already started, and when I went inside I saw Jonah on the floor, a pool of blood around his head. No pulse."

"And what about Gloria?" Callie asked.

"Slumped in a corner, looked like she'd been shot, too, but she was still breathing. I tried to drag her toward the back hallway, but I started choking on the smoke. I was about to pass out, so I figured I'd better get out of there and call for help."

Neither Callie nor Harlan said anything, and she could see that Harlan was running Landry's statement through his mind, trying find holes in it.

"And those shouts you heard," Harlan said. "Right before the gunshots. You know whose they were?"

"Not a clue."

"Male or female?"

"Both, would be my guess."

Callie didn't figure there was much guesswork required. Those voices undoubtedly belonged to Meg Pritchard, Billy Boy Lyman and maybe the third man, who had yet to be identified.

It suddenly occurred to her that they may have misjudged Jonah. Could it be that he had been harboring Meg and her friends against his will? That would explain why he'd come on so strong this afternoon. Maybe he'd had a gun trained on him the whole time.

But then that didn't really fit, did it? Jonah Pritchard had never been a man who was easily intimidated, and she couldn't see Meg and a couple of punks forcing him to do much of anything.

Besides, Jonah had always been Meg's number one apologist. So it seemed more likely that he had welcomed the girl into his home, happy to give her refuge in her time of need, even if she was towing a couple pieces of unwanted baggage along with her.

It looked to Callie as if this was a case of misplaced trust. The question was why had Meg and her friends turned on Jonah? What had gone so horribly wrong?

She doubted Landry would offer any enlightenment. But if anyone could, it was Gloria.

She said to Harlan, "I need to get back to the hospital and talk to Gloria Pritchard."

She turned to go, but Harlan caught her by the crook of the elbow. "Wait a minute."

It had been a very long time since Callie had felt his touch, and she was surprised to find that she recognized it. Remembered it.

Was that even possible?

Gentle yet firm. No intimacy intended, but she suddenly felt as if it were the most intimate thing in the world.

She pulled herself free. "Do you mind?"

"So that's it? You're just gonna take off without me?"

"You didn't seem too anxious to be around me earlier. Besides, this is a murder investigation. Two dead in the span of less than a day, and both murders point to the fire-starting talents of Megan Pritchard-Breen. I hate to break it to you, but your little manhunt is just a sideshow."

"Not if Billy Boy put her up to this."

"You don't know Meg. I can't see anyone calling the shots but her. She's as bullheaded as her grandfather."

"Takes one to know one, I guess."

Callie frowned at him. "What's that supposed to mean?"

"You're about the most bullheaded woman

I've ever met," he said. "Something I used to love about you. Now? Not so much."

Callie's frown deepened. "If this is your way of trying to convince me to let you keep riding shotgun, I think you may want to reconsider your approach."

"At least I didn't call you an idiot."

She huffed at him and started toward her cruiser again, but Harlan caught up to her and once again grabbed her arm. "Callie, I'm not the enemy."

Callie fought off the sudden memory of what he used to do to her with his hands and gave him her best cold stare. "Would you please let go of me?"

He studied her a moment, then did as he was told, Callie saying, "You're on your own from here on out." She continued across the yard, feeling his gaze on her, wishing he would just go away and let her live her life in peace.

But as she climbed into her car and got her seatbelt latched, the passenger door flew open and Harlan sat down next to her.

"I can be bullheaded, too," he said. "So don't even waste your time trying to argue with me."

Chapter Nine

It took an hour and a half of surgery to remove the bullet from Gloria Pritchard's left thigh and get her stitched up. She was still in recovery when they arrived.

The doctor told them they'd have to wait until she was transferred to a room before they could question her. She wouldn't be making much sense until the anesthesia wore off anyway.

"How badly was she hurt?" Callie asked.

"Bullet was a through-and-through. Some muscle and tissue damage, but nothing too serious."

"She got lucky," Harlan said.

The doctor nodded. "She'll be sore for a while, and she may have some problems with her lungs, thanks to smoke inhalation, but she should be back to normal in no time."

Physically, at least, Harlan thought. Mental

and emotional trauma weren't as easy to shake loose. He and Callie were proof of that. And if Gloria's own daughter—or one of her daughter's friends—had done this to her, the condition was likely to be permanent.

As Gloria slept it off in recovery, Callie went to check on her grandmother, leaving Harlan to spend most of the wait alone. He tried to get comfortable on a plastic waiting room chair, but it was an exercise in futility. And after twenty long minutes of staring blankly at a television screen and leafing through old news magazines, Harlan finally got to his feet and headed down the hallway to Callie's grandmother's room.

He may not be wanted, but anything was better than this.

Back in their graduate school days, Callie had spoken fondly about her grandmother, and Harlan knew that the bond between them was unbreakable. But he'd never had the privilege of meeting Mrs. Glass. Had no idea if she even knew he existed.

Still, when Rusty had told him on the phone earlier that she had been hospitalized, he couldn't help feeling some concern. Callie had grown up without her parents, and the thought of losing her grandmother had to be weighing on her mind.

When he reached the doorway, however, he was surprised to find that Callie was nowhere to be found. He thought for a moment that he'd gone to the wrong room, but the woman in the bed looked eerily familiar. A much older, more delicate version of the girl he'd once loved. The ravages of age had done nothing to erase her beauty, and Harlan knew that Callie would grow old just as gracefully. It was in her genes.

Too bad you won't be around to see it.

This thought slipped uninvited into Harlan's brain, and while he wasn't sure where it had come from, he had to admit it was accompanied by a sense of sadness. He had always believed that he and Callie would be together forever, but for some reason fate hadn't been in a cooperative mood.

"Are you gonna stand there daydreaming or say hello?"

Harlan blinked and pulled himself from his thoughts. Callie's grandmother was looking directly at him, a wry smile on her thin face—one that Harlan recognized, although it had been a long time since he'd seen it. Callie didn't seem to smile much nowadays.

"Sorry, ma'am. I was looking for your granddaughter."

"She went out to get me a snack. The food here is horrendous." She gestured to a chair. "You want to sit down?"

"No ma'am, I'll just wait here. I'm Deputy Harlan—"

"Oh, I know who you are. Callie told me you were in town."

Harlan stiffened, half expecting her to start shouting at him for breaking her granddaughter's heart and ruining her life, but the old woman kept right on smiling.

"It was a long time ago," she said, "but every email I got, every phone call that girl made while she was away, she must've mentioned you at least two or three times."

Harlan nodded. "She talked about you a lot, too. I'm sorry we never got a chance to meet."

"So am I."

"We had plans to come up that last summer but...things changed."

Her smile faltered. "Well, I guess that couldn't be helped, could it?"

Harlan shrugged. "*Callie* thinks it could have."

The old woman shook her head. "She's

a complicated girl, that one. So much like her mother, I sometimes find myself wanting to call her Mary. Probably have, once or twice. She makes her mind up about something, she's apt to hang on to it even when she knows she's being unreasonable."

"Well, unreasonable or not, she made up her mind about me. And to be honest, I didn't handle it all that well. Said quite a few things I shouldn't have. And if I'd known what I was walking into when I came here, I probably would've stayed away."

"Now *that* would've been a shame."

The comment surprised Harlan. "Why do you say that?"

The old woman got up on her elbows now, once again looking Harlan straight in the eye. "I know you two have been busy, but in case you haven't noticed, that girl is still in love with you."

Harlan blinked. "I beg your pardon?"

"You heard me. Child likes to pretend she doesn't give two hoots about you, that you're the reason her life went off the rails, yet despite my best efforts over the past decade, she hasn't met a man she can tolerate. And that's all because of you, son."

Harlan's own words about his ex-wife came back to him suddenly.

Because she wasn't you.

Could Callie have been afflicted by the same malady? Was every man she met measured against him? Against what they'd once had?

Not based on what *he'd* seen.

"With all due respect, Mrs. Glass, I think you're dead wrong about that."

She smiled again. "I may be wrong about the weather sometimes, or who's gonna do what to who on my soaps…but I raised that girl and I know her better than anyone alive. And when I say she's still in love with you, you'd better listen carefully, because I don't want you to blow this opportunity."

"Opportunity for what?" Callie said.

She came up behind Harlan, giving him an annoyed look as she squeezed past him through the doorway. She was carrying a bag of takeout.

"What else?" the old woman told her without a hitch. "To help you catch a killer. That *is* why he's here, isn't it? Jonah and I may have had our differences over the years, but it's a shame what happened to him and

Gloria. I guess that's what you get when you raise a bad seed."

"All that stuff I told you is confidential, Nana. I'd appreciate it if you kept it to yourself."

"We're among friends, aren't we?"

Callie shot Harlan a look that pretty much put the lie to everything the old woman had told him. "Colleagues," she corrected. "Even so, you need to learn to watch your tongue. You never know who might be listening."

"I don't think I've revealed any state secrets—have I, Marshal?"

That was a question up for debate, but Harlan said, "No, ma'am."

She looked at Callie. "You see? Always getting hot and bothered over nothing. You need to learn to relax, child."

"And you need to stop telling me that, but I don't suppose you ever will." She turned to Harlan. "Gloria Pritchard's awake and they're moving her to a room. I'll be there in a minute."

Harlan realized this was her not-so-subtle way of telling him to leave, so he nodded to Callie's grandmother. "Nice talking to you, Mrs. Glass."

"Same to you, son. Good to finally meet

you after all these years." She showed him another smile. "Don't let your time here go to waste."

"No, ma'am," he said again. Then he was out the door and gone.

Chapter Ten

Gloria Pritchard was still groggy, but at least she was lucid. Lucid enough to have tears in her eyes.

"I feel so ashamed," she croaked.

"Why's that?" Harlan asked.

He had waited as they got her settled in the room, and by the time the doctor let him in to see her, Callie had shown up, still giving him the cold shoulder—which wasn't a big news flash.

Even so, her grandmother's words kept tumbling through his brain—

That girl is still in love with you.

But Harlan saw no evidence of this himself. Had to believe that the old woman was delusional. He had long ago concluded that it was too late for Callie and him. That the last train had come and gone.

But what if her grandmother was right?

Did he still feel the same about *her*?

Of course you do, you stupid fool. You never stopped *loving her.*

The thought was a revelation, as surprising as the old woman's words, but was it really true? Did being in Callie's presence stir up feelings that had long lain dormant, or was this simply a case of nostalgia? Of regret over things past that merely created the *illusion* that there was still something between them?

Ten years was a long time. Too long to be thinking about trying to rekindle emotions that he couldn't even be sure still existed.

He was out of practice with Callie. The rhythm they'd once had was gone, and if her grandmother's claim was even remotely true, then he obviously didn't know how to read Callie anymore. Because from all appearances, she was done with him. For good.

But enough of this nonsense. He needed to put it aside and concentrate on finding a fugitive.

He returned his attention to Gloria Pritchard as she struggled a moment, then wiped the tears with the back of her hand. "I should have been honest with you this afternoon. If I had, Daddy would probably still be alive."

It was odd hearing her use the term "daddy." Based on her statements that afternoon, Harlan didn't get the impression that the Pritchard household was a particularly loving one.

"Tell us what happened," Callie said. She was in full professional mode, yet Harlan sensed a tension between these two women, the same tension he'd felt when they'd encountered each other that afternoon. There was something going on here that he wasn't privy to.

Gloria closed her eyes, didn't respond. She seemed to be trying to muster up the strength to speak, and he wondered if they'd come here too soon.

But from an investigator's standpoint there was *never* a too soon. Every minute lost was a minute wasted.

Harlan gave her time, then said, "Ms. Pritchard?"

Still no response.

He was about to prompt her again, when she finally opened her eyes and said, "It was Megan. Megan and her friends."

"They came to you for help?"

She nodded. "This morning. She and her friend Billy, and another man named Brett something—I didn't catch his last name."

The potato chip lover.

But Harlan wanted to make sure. Reaching into his inner jacket pocket, he brought out the surveillance photos and showed them to her.

"Are these the men?"

Gloria watched as he leafed through the photos, then squeezed her eyes shut again and nodded. "Yes."

"Did they force their way into your house or did Jonah invite them in?"

She looked at him now. "If you knew Jonah, you wouldn't even have to ask me that question."

"But I *didn't* know him, ma'am, so I'd appreciate it if you'd answer it."

She hesitated, then said, "Jonah worshipped Meg. Loved her more than he ever loved me, that's for sure."

"Even when she brought people like Billy Boy Lyman to the house? He's not exactly what most grandfathers would consider boyfriend material."

"Jonah wasn't your typical grandfather."

"Meaning what?"

"It's no secret what the Pritchard family roots are. Even though we've come a long way, and try to pretend we've elevated ourselves, people around here know exactly what we used to be."

"Which is?"

"Outlaws," Callie told him. "They earned their fortune the easy way."

Gloria looked at her, annoyed. "*Easy* has nothing to do with it. That seed money may have bought our land, but our fortune was built through legitimate hard work." She returned her gaze to Harlan. "My great-grandfather was Jeremiah Pritchard. Before he split off and started his own gang, he used to ride with Robert Leroy Parker."

"You mean Butch Cassidy?" Harlan said.

She nodded. "One of Wyoming's favorite sons. But Jeremiah had his fans, too, and there's no denying he helped turn Williamson into the town it is today."

"Oh, brother," Callie muttered.

Gloria stiffened. The malice in her eyes was hard to disguise. "Poor little Callie. Wants so desperately to be part of this family she can't stand the idea that we've actually accomplished something over the years."

"You have no idea what you're talking about," Callie said.

"Don't I? I know you think that just because your slut mother spread her legs for my brother, that somehow makes you—"

"Shut up," Callie told her, and Harlan could clearly see that Gloria's words had cut very deeply. He thought for a moment he might have to hold Callie back, but she quickly got control of herself.

He had no idea what was going on here. Callie had never once talked about Gloria Pritchard in their time together, but it sounded as if there was a blood connection between these two.

Was Callie Gloria's *niece?*

If so, that would make *Meg* Pritchard her cousin. And that was a clear conflict of interest.

"Is there something we need to talk about?" he said to Callie.

"No. Nothing."

But as much as she tried to hide it, he knew she wasn't being straight with him, and behind the quiet anger there was vulnerability in her eyes. A vulnerability he recognized.

She and Gloria spent the next few seconds

silently eyeballing each other, until Harlan said, "So what are you trying to tell me, Ms. Pritchard? That because you come from outlaw stock that this somehow made Jonah respect a punk like Billy Boy?"

"Jonah grew up worshipping his grandfather and his outlaw ways. He was always drawn to people who rebelled against authority. People like Billy and his friend. And Megan, of course."

"So then what happened? What went wrong?"

"I'm not sure," she said. "I was upstairs and heard them shouting and when I came down to the living room, Meg had a gun pointed at my father."

"And where were Billy Boy and Brett?"

"They were in the room, too. Billy Boy egging her on, telling her to pull the trigger. I think they may have been high."

"And you have no idea what the problem was? Did Meg say anything? Want anything?"

Gloria stiffened. "What difference does it make? She shot him, then turned the gun on me. That's all that matters."

"I'm just trying to make sense of it," Harlan said. "If Jonah admired these people and was willing to help them out of a jam, why would they suddenly turn on the two of you? Why would your own daughter want you dead?"

Gloria averted her gaze now. "I wouldn't know."

"Come on, Ms. Pritchard, your mouth is saying one thing, but your eyes are telling me something else altogether. What happened in that room?"

Gloria was silent. Struggling. Then she said, "I think I'd like to sleep now. Could you two please leave?"

"Not until you've answered the—"

Callie touched his shoulder, stopping him. "It's okay, Harlan. I think I may already know."

He looked at her and saw that her anger had abruptly disappeared, her expression now softened by a mix of surprise and empathy, as if something she had long wondered about suddenly made sense.

He waited for her to continue, but she said nothing, turning instead to Gloria. "The rumors are true, aren't they? About Jonah's...preferences."

Gloria frowned. "What would *you* know about it?"

"This town doesn't have many secrets, Gloria. We've all heard the whispers at one time or another."

"That doesn't mean a damn thing," she snapped. "And it certainly doesn't make it any of your business."

Harlan's voice was gentle but firm. "Look, Ms. Pritchard, I know you're hurting, but a murder victim loses all right to privacy the moment we walk in the door. That's the only way we can build a case against a potential—"

"Go away," she said. "Please."

Harlan took a deep breath, then exhaled. "All right, let's put the motive aside for now. What we really need to know is where Meg and her friends were headed when they left. Did they say anything? Give any indication about where they might be going?"

"Maybe you didn't hear me. I'd like to you leave."

"Not until you tell us—"

"Get out," she shouted. "Get out of my room!"

"Ms. Pritchard—"

"Get out!" She pulled herself upright, her IV rattling, her face turning crimson. Tears filled her eyes, spilling down her cheeks as

she continued to shout at them. "*Leave* me alone!"

Whatever she was hiding, it was ugly and painful, so painful that she seemed unaware of the wound in her thigh which was starting to bleed, staining her blankets.

Harlan and Callie backed away from her now as the room began to fill with hospital personnel, people in scrubs telling them to go, *now,* as they moved to the bed to try to calm Gloria down.

And as he and Callie retreated into the hallway, Harlan could only thank God that the troubles he'd seen in his own life seemed tame in comparison to what this woman must be going through. The memories they had triggered were ripping her up inside, and even though it couldn't be helped, he felt a twinge of guilt for pushing her.

He looked at Callie, saw the dismay on her face, and thought she must be thinking the very same thing. And despite all they'd been through in their time, Harlan suddenly realized that they were the lucky ones.

Very lucky indeed.

Chapter Eleven

"That went well," Harlan said. "You want to clarify for me what just happened back there?"

Callie felt sick to her stomach. There had long been rumors about Jonah Pritchard, but she'd never really believed them. She had always thought it was nothing more than vicious small town gossip, whipped up out of boredom and envy.

Yet Gloria's reaction to their questioning seemed to be confirmation of those rumors. Which would explain Megan Pritchard's rebelliousness over the span of her life. If Meg had finally had enough of her grandfather's "attention," then that would surely be a motive to pick up a gun and shoot the old man.

But what about Gloria? Was she complicit in her father's crimes? Is that why she'd reacted so violently? If so, then it was no wonder that she'd been shot as well.

Callie's gut churned. The thought that she shared DNA with these people made her want to throw up.

She and Harlan were back in her SUV, headed to the ranch to pick up Harlan's cruiser, his question still hanging in the air.

"Well?" he said.

"You're a reasonably intelligent man," she told him. "I think you can figure it out."

He shook his head in disgust. "I was hoping I was wrong. Makes me feel a little guilty for pushing her buttons like that."

"Imagine how *I* feel."

He turned to her now, those blue eyes of his studying her as she gripped the wheel. "Gloria isn't the only one keeping secrets, is she?"

"It isn't exactly a secret. It's just not something I talk about."

"Are you ready to talk about it *now?*"

She shrugged. "There isn't much to tell. My mother and Gloria's brother were an item in high school, and she and Gloria were best friends. Until she got pregnant, that is."

"And that was your *mother's* fault, right?"

"Gloria thought so, and never forgave her

for it. She looks at me and all she sees is the reason her brother is dead."

"Why? What happened to him?"

"Jonah made him enlist in the army when they found out my mom was pregnant and he got killed in a truck accident. Which is a shame, because Nana Jean says he was the only decent Pritchard this side of Sheridan. Didn't have that air of entitlement the rest of them do. It would've been nice to have gotten to know the man."

Callie had never really missed her parents because she'd grown up without them, but she did sometimes let the "what ifs" occupy her mind.

She looked at Harlan and couldn't be sure, but thought he might be upset by these revelations.

"Is something wrong?"

He shook his head. "It's just that I can't believe we were together for nearly two and a half years and you never said a word to me about any of this."

"It didn't really affect us, and I didn't want to burden you with my family drama."

"That's just it," he said. "It wouldn't have been a burden. I was in love with you, Callie.

I wanted to know everything there was to know about you."

She looked at him again—at those blue eyes still fixed on her—and she remembered that beneath his hard exterior he had always had a soft heart. Gentle. Empathetic.

He'd been a kind lover, too. Aggressive but never rough, and always attentive to her needs, physically and emotionally. So of *course* he would want to know everything about her.

That was who Harlan *was*.

Remembering this, Callie felt her heart kick up. She had been in love, too. The kind of love that made her anxious to wake up every morning. To see him. Touch him. Feel the embrace of those eyes. Those lips.

Those hands.

She missed that feeling. Missed the comfort of it. The excitement.

But after Treacher had been killed, all of that had stopped. Grief had consumed her, made her impossible to be around. The circumstances surrounding his death had made her cruel and judgmental and inconsolable. She hadn't wanted Harlan anywhere near her.

Who would have thought that the loss of

a close friend could do that to her? To them? Yet it had. And in the process she'd not only lost someone she'd thought of as a brother, but also the man she loved.

Two for the price of one.

Returning her attention to the road, she wondered why she still felt so angry at Harlan.

Did he really deserve her scorn?

Wasn't it time to forgive and forget?

Her feelings for him hadn't vanished— anyone paying close attention knew that. Otherwise she'd be indifferent to him, un-willing to waste any mental bandwidth thinking about him. And it was becoming more and more apparent that Harlan was using up the majority of that bandwidth.

She simply had no choice in the matter.

No choice at all.

Harlan sobered and said, "I guess there's no point in dwelling on the past, is there?"

"I try not to."

"But based on what you've told me, I think you need to consider removing yourself from this case."

Cue the record scratch.

Callie swiveled her head toward him. *"What?"*

"One of the perpetrators is your cousin, Callie. The victim is your aunt. I felt the tension between you two even before Gloria went ballistic. If you keep going like this, your judgment could be impaired."

Callie couldn't quite believe what she was hearing.

So much for forgiving and forgetting.

"You have got to be kidding me."

"It doesn't help that you and I aren't exactly a loving couple anymore. We probably shouldn't even be working together."

"You were the one who wanted to tag along, remember? You can leave anytime you want to."

"I'm serious, Callie."

"So am I."

Harlan sighed. "Look, maybe you and your boss don't see it, but there's a clear conflict of interest here and your involvement in this case is just a bad idea all around."

All right. Enough was enough.

Without even thinking about it, Callie suddenly slammed the brakes, bringing the SUV to a hard stop in the middle of the road.

"Get out of the car," she said.

"What?"

"You heard me."

"You're being ridiculous."

"Maybe you haven't noticed, Harlan, but this isn't Colorado, and there's only one person in this case who falls under your jurisdiction. Billy Boy Lyman. So why don't you concentrate on catching him and leave the rest to the Williamson County Sheriff's Office."

She reached to the armrest and popped the locks on the doors. "Now get out of the car."

MOMENTS AFTER LEAVING Harlan in the middle the road, Callie started having second thoughts.

What was she doing?

Her actions only proved that he was right about this. That she was too emotionally involved to make smart, rational judgments. Leaving him stranded was not only childish, it was unbecoming of a Williamson County Sheriff's deputy. A senior one, at that.

As Harlan shrank to a pinprick in her rearview mirror, Callie made a vow not to let him get under her skin, then eased off the accelerator and made a quick U-turn.

A moment later she was pulling up alongside him, once again popping the locks as she rolled down her window.

"I'm sorry. That was a stupid thing to do."

Harlan shrugged it off. "We all do stupid things. I shouldn't have been so quick to judge you."

"The problem is, you're right," she said. "I *should* recuse myself." She smiled tersely. "But I'm not going to."

He didn't seem surprised. "You wouldn't be the Callie Glass I once knew and loved if you did."

They both let that percolate for a moment, then she gestured. "So are you just going to stand there gawking at me or get back in the car?"

He gave her a salute, then moved around to the passenger side and climbed in next to her.

They said nothing as she made another U-turn and headed toward Pritchard Ranch. The Bighorn Mountains loomed beyond— a dark, jagged line silhouetted against the night sky.

She thought back to what Gloria had said about her great-grandfather being an outlaw. When Callie was a child, she had heard stories about Jeremiah Pritchard and his gang of thieves roaming these mountains. He was often called the Robin Hood of Williamson

County, using the money he'd robbed from banks and trains to help his friends buy land in the area, long before Williamson was what it was today.

It was a legend the Pritchards had traded on for decades. And Callie, knowing that she, too, was related to Jeremiah, had sometimes imagined herself riding with the gang, robbing banks, running from the law and...

A sudden thought occurred to her. "Oh, my God," she murmured.

Harlan turned. "What?"

"I think I may know where our fugitives went."

Harlan's eyebrows raised. "What? Where?"

Callie punched the accelerator and blasted down the road, taking the curve toward Pritchard Ranch. A few moments later she pulled through the gate to find Harlan's cruiser and only a single fire truck parked in front of the smoldering remnants of the house. She pulled in next to the cruiser and killed the engine.

Unlatching her glove compartment, she pulled out a flashlight and said, "Follow me."

Then she had her door open and was out of the SUV, Harlan moving alongside her as she crossed past the fire truck, then flicked on the flashlight and headed down a sloping patch of lawn toward a large wooden structure sitting a few hundred yards away.

"The stable?" Harlan said. "The place has already been searched, top to bottom."

"I know," Callie told him, "but they were searching for the wrong thing."

"What do you mean?"

"They were searching for people."

They reached the stable and Callie threw open the doors, shining her flashlight around until she found a light switch mounted on a wooden post inside. She flicked the switch and overhead fluorescents came to life.

The stable was empty. No sign of any livestock.

"Remember what Landry told us?" Callie said. "That he was feeding the horses when the fire started?"

"Yeah, what about it?"

Callie gestured. "So do you see any horses here?"

Harlan looked around. "You think he was lying?"

Callie shook her head. "This is the Pritchard's private stable, remember? Which means Meg would likely have a horse housed here, along with Gloria's and Jonah's rides.

And it looks like someone took them after Landry ran up to the house. Three fugitives, three horses."

Harlan was skeptical. "Or he could've left the doors open and the horses got spooked. They could be anywhere."

"There's one way to find out."

Callie pulled out her cell phone and dialed. A moment later, Rusty was on the line. "Wilcox."

"Rusty, this is Callie. Where'd they take Landry Bickham after we left?"

"Sheriff Mercer released him. He didn't have a place to stay, so I drove him to the Cottonwood Motel."

"Do me a favor and call him over there, then call me back and put us on conference."

"What's going on?"

"I'll explain later," she said, then hung up.

As they waited for the return call, Harlan moved around the stable, poking his head into the empty stalls. Callie watched him, once again thinking how well he had aged. Thinking how he still had that fluid, effort-less way of moving, as if he were completely in tune with his body.

Then her cell phone rang, interrupting the thought, and she clicked it on. "Glass."

"Hey, Callie, I've got Landry on the line."

"Thanks, Rusty. Can you hear me, Landry?"

"I hear you," a familiar voice said, and he didn't sound happy. "And I'm seriously thinking about filing a lawsuit for harassment."

"Oh, grow up. I just need you to answer one more question."

He sighed. "Which is?"

"When you heard the gunshots and ran up to the house, did you leave any of the stable doors open?"

"Of course I didn't."

"You sure? Even in the heat of the moment?"

"Is that some kind of sick joke?"

She saw his point, but didn't feel like dealing with his nonsense. "Landry, will you please just answer the—"

"No," he said. "Not even in the heat of the moment. You work for the Pritchards, you learn good habits or you'll be looking for another job. Doesn't matter what's goin' on around you, closing up the stable is second nature, like zipping up your fly after you've done your business."

Thanks for the visual, Callie thought.

"And the horses were here when you left?"

"Of course they were. I said I was feeding 'em, didn't I? What's this all about?"

"Stay on the line a minute. Rusty, you there?"

"I'm here," Rusty said.

"Is Katie Patterson still head honcho over at the Williamson County Library?"

"I think so," he said.

"Good. I need you to track her down and get to the library ASAP. And swing by the Cottonwood and take Landry with you."

"Me?" Landry said. "What do you need me for?"

"Your expertise," Callie told him, then disconnected before he could object.

Pocketing her phone, she turned to find Harlan hovering nearby, not hiding his curiosity. "You ready tell me what you're up to?"

"I already told you," she said. "Finding our fugitives."

Chapter Twelve

Katie Patterson was not what most people thought of when you said the word *librarian*. At fifty-four she was a twice-divorced bottle blonde with a raucous, tobacco-tinged laugh that had taken more than a few of her patrons by surprise.

Most of her nights were spent at a bar in town called Little Pete's where she regularly debated politics, sports and religion. And if the right man made the right moves, she sometimes wound up sleeping in a bed other than her own.

Katie didn't look, act or talk the way you'd expect a librarian to, but she did have three important things going for her. She was smart as a whip, did her job better than any of her predecessors and everybody in town just plain loved her.

"Got it all right here," she said as she

emerged from a hallway at the rear of the Williamson County Library. It was long past business hours, but she had been happy to open the place up, especially after she found out she'd be helping in an investigation. "Everything there is to know about the Pritchard gang, all in one box."

She let out a husky laugh and dropped a large storage box on the table in front of them. Callie, Harlan, Rusty, Landry and Sheriff Mercer all watched as she pulled the lid off to reveal several documents, yellowed by time, along with a stack of folded maps and an envelope full of archival photographs.

Callie immediately reached for the envelope and opened it.

"You know what you're looking for?" Katie asked.

"Photo I remember seeing when I was a little girl. Pritchard posing for a local photographer."

"That would be Terrance Scarne," Katie said. "Those are his photos hanging in City Hall. He chronicled the history of Williamson for nearly five decades."

Anyone who had gone in to renew their driver's license had seen those photographs. Stark black and white shots of horses and buggies on unpaved streets, back when Williamson was little more than a shanty town.

Callie found what she was looking for and said, "Here it is," then showed the photo to the rest of the group.

It was a posed shot of a tall, unshaven man wearing a dark hat, vest and dungarees, a six shooter slung on his hip as he stared unsmiling into the camera. In the distance behind him was a large wooden cabin, smoke billowing up from a chimney into a cloudless Wyoming sky.

"Jeremiah Pritchard," Katie said. "The Robin Hood of Williamson County."

Harlan didn't seem impressed. "Fascinating. But I'm not quite sure why we're looking at it."

Katie frowned. "This is history, son. Don't need a *reason* to be looked at."

"Unless you have one," Callie said, then pointed to a handwritten caption in the lower right corner:

ROBBERS CANYON 1887

"Is that something significant?" Harlan asked.

Callie nodded. "Robbers Canyon was the

Pritchard gang's hideout in the Bighorn Mountains. Nobody outside the family knows where this photo was taken, but some people say the Pritchards have kept the place in good repair. That Jonah would go there sometimes and spend the night, soak in the ambience. Which isn't surprising when you consider his love of his outlaw heritage." She paused, looked at Landry. "I'm betting *you* know something about it, too."

Landry's trademark smile had apparently taken the night off. "Is that what you dragged me here for?"

"I brought you here because I think you're lying to us. I think you know full well that Megan and Billy Boy Lyman were in that house, and this is where they went." She tapped the image of the cabin for emphasis.

Landry scoffed. "If that was true, why wouldn't I tell you? According to Rusty here, they're the ones killed Jonah."

"And I imagine that's troubling to you," Callie said, "but your loyalties aren't just to the old man. You're so used to protecting the Pritchard family secrets that you're no doubt feeling pretty conflicted right now."

She could see that conflict in his eyes, but he was so deeply indoctrinated that he wasn't about to admit it. Not out loud. "You're out of your mind."

"There's no shame in feeling this way, Landry. You've been with that family your entire life. Your own kin used to ride with Jeremiah Pritchard and you've seen them through births and deaths and divorces, all the time doing what you could to help them out." She paused. "But even Gloria herself says her daughter's out of control. She's the one who told us Meg pulled the trigger."

A flicker of surprise replaced the conflict, but it quickly disappeared. "I don't have to listen this," Landry said, then started away from the table.

Harlan grabbed him by the forearm. "Hold on, Bickham, not so fast. I don't think she's finished."

Landry wasn't a small man, but Harlan didn't seem too concerned about his size. He swung him back around to the table and nudged him forward.

"Floor is yours," he said the Callie.

Callie reached into the box and pulled out the stack of folded maps. There were dates penciled in the corner of each. She found one dated 1888 and unfolded it onto the table.

It was hand drawn, showing Williamson

and the surrounding area from a time nearly forgotten, including the acreage that comprised Pritchard Ranch and a good portion of the Bighorn Mountains.

She pointed to those mountains. "Now I know that people have long speculated where Jeremiah's hideout may be, but those who've been adventurous enough to try to find it have never been successful." She looked up at Landry. "But I think you've been there with Jonah. And I think you know exactly where it is."

He eyed her defiantly. "So what if I do?"

Callie smiled. "You're going tell us how to get there."

IT TOOK LANDRY A WHILE to break, but with Harlan once again threatening to arrest him for aiding and abetting a fugitive he finally gave in. He refused to admit any knowledge that the trio had gone to Robbers Canyon—or that they'd been to the Pritchard Ranch at all—but with great reluctance he dropped a finger to the map and showed Callie and the others how to get there.

What they learned was that the trail to Robbers Canyon was nearly a day-long trek, and could only be accessed on horseback.

Sheriff Mercer mentioned the possibility of going in by chopper, but Landry assured him that a helicopter wouldn't have a place to land. Besides, Harlan told them, even if it did, the noise would give them away and they'd lose the element of surprise. Not something he was willing to risk.

"Which once again leaves us with you," Callie said to Landry.

"Meaning what?"

"You can be our guide. Take us in there nice and quiet."

Landry balked. "Now, hold on. I already told you how to get there, and that's about all I've got to offer. You can't force me to go along, and I'm not about to volunteer, so you're on your own from here on out." He looked at Harlan. "And if you wanna throw me in the bucket, so be it. Couldn't be any worse than the Cottonwood Inn."

"How about if we paid you?" Mercer said.

"Paid me?"

"With Jonah dead, you might be looking for a job. Not a place you want to be in this tight economy, and I'm sure we could scrounge up a little cash for your services."

Landry shook his head. "With all due respect, Sheriff, I'd just as soon take money from the devil himself."

Which, to Callie's mind, was exactly what he'd been doing all along.

Why change now?

THEY MADE PLANS TO LEAVE first thing in the morning. Sheriff Mercer, who had a small stable of his own, promised to bring the horses, and they arranged a rendezvous for seven o'clock at Pritchard Ranch.

That would leave Callie just enough time to swing by the bakery and pick up Nana's muffins. She felt a little guilty about taking a trek into the wilderness on the day the doctors would be poking and prodding the old woman, but Nana understood the nature of Callie's job and would insist she go. Besides, Judith would be happy to play stand-in.

As Callie and Harlan headed out to their cars, Harlan said, "Good thinking in there."

They were being cordial now, and she wasn't quite used to it. Had to readjust a little. "Thanks."

"Sheriff says all the road blocks have come up empty, so I'm pretty sure you're right about this. Makes sense that Billy Boy would want to lay low for a few weeks, in hopes we'll get tired of looking for him."

"As if *that* would ever happen."

Harlan grinned. "Billy Boy Lyman has the intelligence and foresight of a two-year-old child."

Callie gestured to the bruise on the side of his face. "That didn't stop him from putting one over on *you*."

It was a good-natured jab and Harlan took it that way. "I'm laying this one on cousin Meg. I knew she was a force to be reckoned with the minute I walked into that convenience store. I figure she's the one dreamed up Lyman's escape."

"Nobody's ever accused her of being dumb, that's for sure. And if they *are* at that hideout, somebody had to give them supplies."

"You thinking Landry?"

She shrugged. "He was awfully reluctant to help us. And considering Gloria gave Meg up to us in about ten seconds flat, I don't think she's the one."

"Could be Jonah had them set to go before things got ugly."

"True. He would've done anything for that girl. Maybe they had this whole thing figured out days ago. Billy Boy's escape, the trip up to the hideout. But I don't think killing Jim Farber was part of the plan, and that could be another reason Jonah and Meg got into it. He probably didn't know about the murder until I told him."

Harlan nodded agreement. "Whatever the case, I'd bet a month's salary they're stoking up that cabin's fireplace as we speak."

"No doubt," Callie said.

They were quiet for a moment, then Harlan broke off and stepped toward his cruiser. "Wouldn't mind stoking up a fireplace myself. I could fall asleep right in front of it."

"You have a place to stay?"

"I thought I'd head over to that motel. The Cottonwood?"

Callie nodded, then took her keys out and opened up her SUV. She was about to get inside, when she stopped herself, hoping she wasn't making a mistake.

She said to Harlan, "I've been pretty hostile to you and I'm sorry about that."

"I haven't exactly been Mr. Agreeable."

"I hate to see you stuck in a place like the Cottonwood. Why don't you come on over to the house? We've got a guest room you can use."

Harlan looked surprised. "You sure you want to do that?"

"No," she said, "but I'm doing it anyway. You're just lucky Nana won't be there."

"Why's that?"

"She'd be trying to get us all to sit down for tea and sandwiches."

Harlan laughed. "Well, in that case I think I'll take you up on your offer." He gave her an imaginary tip of the hat. "Thank you, kindly, ma'am."

Callie suddenly felt something warm stir inside her. The hat tip was a gesture that the old Harlan made on a pretty regular basis. It was his ode to John Wayne, one of his heroes.

On their first date he'd taken Callie to a revival of the Western *McClintock*. They'd only been study friends until then, but halfway through the movie she saw Harlan quietly mouthing one of The Duke's lines—"You have to be a man before you can be a gentleman"—and she knew she was in love.

She had put her hand in his and leaned her head on his shoulder, and before the night was over, she lay for the first time in his bed, exhilarated by his touch and his complete lack of selfishness. She discovered very quickly that he was both a man *and* a gentleman.

As Callie thought about this, however, the warmth she felt gave way to sadness.

How could she have let that go?

How could she have let any of it go?

"Shall we take your car?" Harlan asked. "Or do you want me to follow you?"

She pulled herself from her thoughts. "I'll drive," she said, then climbed in behind the wheel.

Chapter Thirteen

Harlan didn't quite know what to make of Callie's invitation. The move was unexpected. But then he thought again about what her grandmother had said.

She's still in love with you, you know.

Was there any truth to that?

Part of him wanted to believe it, but a bigger part had serious doubts. She was simply being kindhearted, because, beneath it all, that was Callie. She may have had her stubborn streak, and that hair-trigger temper, but the woman he'd known had been a nurturer at heart. Offering up her spare bedroom was just the kind of thing she'd do. So there was no point in reading anything into it.

Besides, why should it matter to him? He and Callie were long done, and he had his own life in Colorado Springs. True, he'd kept his relationships casual since his divorce, but he didn't often fret over his life as a single man.

He had freedom, could come and go as he pleased. And coming home to an empty apartment was something he'd gotten used to.

But if he was entirely honest with himself, there were nights he'd walk into that apartment and yearn. Not for his ex-wife—that had been a mistake. And not for any of the women he was currently dating.

But for Callie. For that feeling they'd once shared. As if their souls had somehow been connected.

Those were the times he'd root around in his kitchen cupboard until he found a bottle of Jack Daniels. He'd quietly get drunk as he watched the night sky, thinking about all the things he should have said and done back when Treacher was killed. But he'd been too young and stupid—Billy Boy Lyman stupid—and he'd let grief devour him, just as it had devoured Callie.

Harlan sometimes hated Treacher for what he'd done to them, for his irresponsibility. Couldn't he see how much in love they were? What made him think he had the right to destroy that with his reckless behavior?

But if Harlan got drunk enough, he sometimes wondered if Callie had been right. If he'd been more forceful, if he hadn't been distracted by a woman—a major bone of contention with Callie—Treacher never would've gotten behind the wheel of that car and would probably be alive today.

If, if, if...

Sometimes on those nights Harlan saw his best friend smiling at him from beyond the stars, and all the promise in that youthful, charismatic face. And sure enough, Harlan would find himself crying. Drunken tears, but tears nevertheless. Something he didn't like to admit to, but he figured you weren't really a man if you didn't know how to let it loose now and again.

So he let it loose, mourning his losses like a child who has finally realized that his runaway dog isn't ever coming home again.

And the hardest part of all was knowing that when he woke up in the morning, his apartment would still be empty.

HARLAN WAS THINKING about these things as they pulled into to Callie's driveway.

"Home sweet home," she said, setting the parking brake.

He studied the house, a modest one-story

structure with a rustic feel. It *looked* liked home. Comfortable. Aged, but well-tended.

"You were born here, weren't you?"

"Probably die here, too," Callie said. "This house and Nana Jean are the only constants in my life." She paused. "And the job, of course."

"Of course. The all-consuming beast."

She smiled. "But in a good way."

"Tell that to my face," he said, gesturing to the bruise.

They both laughed as they opened their doors and climbed out, and it was good to hear Callie laughing. There had always been a bright, musical quality to the sound that lifted his spirits. And they needed lifting right now.

Callie jangled her keys and let him in through the front door, then they moved together through a small parlor into a modestly appointed living room, Callie flicking the lights on as they went.

"The spare bedroom is in back," she said, then gestured to a stone fireplace in a corner of the room. "Or you can start that fire you wanted and sleep on the sofa. Your choice."

"No contest," he told her. "Fire it is. As long as I don't wind up like Jonah Pritchard."

"Ugh," Callie said, then pushed him away.

"Bad taste? Too soon?"

"Way too soon."

"So I suppose if I say I want Rice Crispies for breakfast, you'll throw me out of your house?"

He could see that she was about to laugh again, which, of course, was what he'd been hoping for. Cops weren't known for their tasteful humor, and Harlan wasn't any exception. The kind of job they did, humor was often their only relief. Even if it was a bit morbid.

But before he could say anything more, she seemed to sense he was about to crack another joke, and held up a finger.

"Stop," she said, stifling the laugh. "Keep your mouth shut and get to work. I'll grab you some blankets."

So Harlan did as he was told and moved over to the stack of wood next to the fireplace. Shoving aside the grate, he stacked several pieces inside, turned on the gas, then took a long-nosed utility lighter from a basket next to the wood and lit the fire.

It would be a few minutes before the wood caught and he could turn off the gas, so he moved to a rack on a nearby wall that held several bottles of wine. He found a nice Pinot and held it up as Callie came back into the room carrying two blankets and a pillow.

"Quick drink before bed?" he asked.

One of Callie's eyebrows went up. "This isn't a date, Harlan. Don't take this offer the wrong way."

"How could I?" he said. "You're always pretty clear about what you think and feel."

"Maybe not clear enough. Just because we've decided to be cordial doesn't mean this is anything more than two colleagues—"

"It's just wine, Callie."

She caught herself. Smiled. "I guess I've always been too serious for my own good. I'll get the glasses."

She dropped the pillow and blankets on the sofa, then disappeared into the kitchen as Harlan found a corkscrew and opened the bottle.

A moment later she came back and held out the glasses as he poured, a little more generous with the liquid than he needed to be. Truth was, Harlan was disappointed by her insistence that this meant nothing, even though he'd suspected as much. He couldn't stop staring at her, thinking about her body, the way she carried herself. Remembering the things they used to do together. Alone. On his bed.

Maybe the wine would dull his senses a bit.

"To tracking down bad guys," he said, punctuating the words by touching his glass to hers, marveling at how beautiful she looked in the growing firelight.

She stood only inches from him now and he wanted so much to lean forward and kiss her, to taste her lips. But he knew that would be a serious mistake. Instead he drank his wine, nearly downing it in a single gulp.

Callie said, "Slow down, partner, that isn't grape juice."

He finished it off and wiped his mouth with the back of his hand. "I guess I needed that more than I thought I did."

Then he looked into her eyes again and thought he saw a flicker of desire there. A look he'd seen many times before.

But he couldn't be sure. Especially now that the wine was flowing through his bloodstream. He hadn't been lying about the transparency of her emotions, so maybe what he saw was only the flicker of the fire playing tricks on him. Or his own desire getting the better of him.

He poured another finger of liquid and downed it, then turned and set the glass and bottle on a nearby end table. The wood in the fireplace had caught now, and he crossed to the gas valve and shut it off.

"Guess we'd better get some sleep," he said. "Thanks again for putting me up." He smiled. "And for putting up with me."

"Not so hard," she said. "I deal with criminals for a living, remember?"

Then she finished her glass, set in on the table next to his and bid him goodnight as she left the room.

Harlan didn't think he'd ever been so sorry to see someone go.

It was closing in on three o'clock when Harlan heard the sound.

The sofa was comfortable enough, and although the fire had died down quite a bit, he could feel its warmth. But he'd slept fitfully through the night, still thinking about Callie and his desire to kiss her. To take her in his arms.

He couldn't decide if what he was feeling was real and immediate, or simply the residue of a past that hadn't been completely scrubbed away.

Get a grip on yourself, moron. You're here to do a job and nothing—

The sound came from a hallway on his left—the faint padding of footsteps on wood, and he realized he had dozed off for a moment.

He turned now and saw her silhouetted against what was left of the fire, and in the faint light could see that she was wearing an oversize University of Colorado sweatshirt. Probably the same one she used to wear in the old days. It cut high on her thighs, her smooth bare legs exposed to the night air.

She looked as if she hadn't aged a day since college, and if he wasn't mistaken, there were tears in her eyes.

"I can't sleep," she said softly.

"Neither can I."

Without another word she climbed onto the sofa next to him, pressing her warm body against his, leaning in to kiss him.

As she opened her mouth, the faint smell of her breath wafted past him—a uniquely *Callie* scent that he would know with his eyes closed. Their lips touched and he drew her tongue in, the taste as sweet and inviting as he remembered.

And as they kissed, she snaked a hand

down past the blankets, sliding her fingers across the fabric of his boxers until she found him and gently squeezed.

There are those who think that sex is just sex for a man, that he'll sleep with any women he finds remotely attractive. But this wasn't true for Harlan. He wasn't a monk, that was certain, but in all the years they'd been apart he had never found a woman who excited him the way Callie did. He instantly grew hard against her hand, the sudden need to be inside her nearly overwhelming in its intensity.

He wanted to feel her heat envelope him, the memory of it quickening his pulse. He rolled her over onto the cushions and pressed himself against her. Pushing her sweatshirt up, he gently took hold of her right breast and ran his thumb across the nipple, feeling it harden at the touch. Then he lowered he lips to it and she arched her back slightly, pressing into him, her hands searching again, reaching past the elastic of his boxers until she found him.

And he knew that she was feeling the very same overwhelming need. The all-consuming desire. It was as if they had been in a constant state of foreplay ever since he walked into that conference room. He wanted to take his time to please her, but she seemed to be well beyond such concerns, the urgency of her breathing telling him that she was ready for him. Now.

Moving her hands to his waistband again, she pushed his shorts down to free him. She was wearing a pair of silky panties, but she didn't bother to remove them. Instead she pulled them to one side and guided him into her, kissing him, whispering in his ear, "I'm sorry. I'm so sorry."

"No," he said. "It's my fault. It was all my fault."

And he thrust forward like man possessed, electric heat radiating through his body as she writhed beneath him, mewing and moaning with each powerful thrust. He scraped his teeth across her shoulder, her neck, then found her mouth and her tongue again, her quickening breaths in perfect counterpoint to his moving hips.

And just as he thought he couldn't take any more, as if his mind were about to succumb to an explosion of ecstasy, she suddenly looked up at him and said, "Wake up, Harlan. We need to get moving."

Harlan blinked, opened his eyes. Found

himself alone on the sofa, his legs tangled in the blankets.

Callie was standing across the room in the kitchen doorway, dressed and ready for work, a cup of coffee in hand.

"You seemed to be having a heck of a nightmare," she said. "You want to share?"

Harlan blinked again, trying to get his bearings. "Did we…? Did…"

"What?"

And then the realization that it had all been a dream came crashing in on him.

"Never mind," he croaked.

"Are you okay?" Callie asked.

Still trying to get his bearings, Harlan nodded. "Fine… I'm… I'm fine."

"Then hurry up and shower. I want to swing by and see Nana before we meet Rusty and Mercer."

Harlan shifted uncomfortably on the sofa. *Easier said than done,* he thought.

It would be a while before he could stand up without embarrassing himself.

Chapter Fourteen

"You sure you're okay?" Callie asked.

Whatever Harlan had seen in his dream must have rattled him. He'd been acting funny all morning.

They had been waiting near the charred remnants of the Pritchard house for a good fifteen minutes now, and he'd barely said a word to her since they'd left the house.

"Harlan?"

"Sheriff's here."

He nodded to a truck pulling a long horse trailer as it turned into the drive, Mercer behind the wheel, Rusty riding shotgun. Mercer brought it to a stop and they climbed out, greeting Callie and Harlan with grim nods.

Nobody was looking forward to this ride.

"You try Landry again?" she asked Mercer.

"I would have if he was still around."

Mercer dug into his shirt pocket, produced a wooden matchstick, and stuck it between his lips. He'd been trying to quit smoking for weeks. "Hank over at the Cottonwood says he checked out first thing this morning. No mention of where he was headed."

"He didn't look too happy when we left last night."

Mercer chewed on the matchstick as he moved around toward the rear of the horse trailer. "Can't say I blame him. He's known Meg since the day she was born, so I can understand why he'd be reluctant to help us."

Landry was too loyal for his own good. Callie figured he'd spent all these years tending to Jonah Pritchard's every wish, and what had he gotten out of it? She couldn't imagine that he was in Jonah's will. The ranch and the Pritchard fortune would undoubtedly be inherited by Gloria and Meg, and Landry would be left out in the cold.

But Mercer was right. The poor smiling fool felt indebted to the Pritchards and it had been a stretch to think he'd help any more than he already had. Mapping out the trail to the Pritchard gang's old hideout was enough of a betrayal to last him a lifetime.

And Callie wouldn't be surprised if he was busy getting an early-morning drunk on.

Mercer took a mobile GPS device from his pocket. "We get up high enough in those mountains, this thing won't be worth squat."

"Terrific," Callie muttered.

The world had grown dependent on satellites and electronic gadgets, and map or no map, she knew this trek wouldn't be an easy one.

Mercer had initially considered attempting an all-out assault, using every deputy he had available to him, but before they'd left the library last night they had decided to keep the team lean and mean. The less manpower involved, the faster they could move.

So it was just the four of them.

This particular stretch of the Bighorns, however, was known to be treacherous territory, which was why a band of outlaws had been attracted to it over a century ago. That it hadn't changed was a testament to how dangerous it could be.

"The main thing we have to remember," Mercer continued, "is to stick together. I don't want anyone getting lost up there."

"Maybe we should try a little harder to find *Landry*," Rusty said. "Appeal to his sense of civic duty."

"Good luck with that."

Fortunately, they were all experienced riders. Landry had furnished them with plenty of landmarks and both Rusty and Callie had done group hikes in these mountains. But today they'd be going well beyond the established trails and once they got into no-man's-land, they'd have be doubly careful.

The only Bighorns virgin in the group was Harlan, but he had assured them he'd be able to hold his own. And despite his odd behavior this morning, Callie didn't doubt it for a minute. She might have her issues with the guy, but he'd always been strong and capable and smart.

"We're wasting time," he said. "What do you say we saddle up and get moving?"

Mercer unlatched the gate of his trailer. The horses—four Morgans from his personal stable—were huffing and shuffling restlessly inside, anxious to be let free. It was a breed Mercer had always sworn by, telling Callie that they were the best trail mounts a man could ask for.

"I think these gals kinda like that idea," he said.

THE BIGHORN MOUNTAINS were a stretch of the Rockies that spanned two states—north-central Wyoming and southern Montana. The range was a well-known tourist destination for campers, hikers and riders alike, and there were lodges and trails and campgrounds available to anyone with an adventurous streak.

The trail Callie and company were following, however, was not one that was often used. The late Jonah Pritchard had seen to that. It started at the northern part of his property and snaked a good distance up toward Cloud Peak, through what was commonly known as the Cloud Peak Wilderness. The area was controlled by the National Forest Service, but never tell a Pritchard that. Their sense of entitlement stretched well beyond the boundries of any federal mandate.

Robbers Canyon was hidden deep within that wilderness, beyond what anyone familiar with the Pritchard gang legend called the Lost Woods, where the gang had outmaneuvered and sometimes outgunned many a posse.

Callie and the others rode single file along the winding trail, Mercer in the lead, consulting his GPS for as long as it would let him. They all had compasses and photocopies of Landry's hand-drawn map, in case one of them got lost, but so far they were relying on modern technology to get them there.

That would change soon enough, but for the first few hours of the ride, Mercer had shown the way.

As the day wore on, Callie's seat bones started feeling a little sore. It had been a good year since she'd ridden a horse, and not only did she feel it in her butt, she knew that her thigh muscles would pay for it dearly. The ache would set in the minute she dismounted.

Which was bound to be soon, she thought. They'd been riding for over half the day now, mostly uphill, and the horses needed some rest.

As if reading her mind, Mercer called back to them, "There's a creek just around this bend. Might be a good time to water the horses."

"Can't that wait?" Rusty asked. "The sooner were get there the better."

"These gals may be tough, but they need their rest, and I don't figure our fugitives are going anywhere. We'll get there soon enough."

A moment later they rounded the bend and crossed toward a narrow creek that wound past a steep, rocky hillside. They cued their horses to a stop, then dismounted and led them to the water, Callie feeling a burn in her thigh muscles that she knew would be even worse tomorrow. Her legs were trembling slightly, as if she'd just spent the past couple hours making love.

If only.

As Mercer tended to the horses, Rusty found some shade under a nearby tree, then sat down and leaned his back against it, fanning himself. "Could anyone else go for a nice cold beer right now?"

Harlan was still uncharacteristically silent. Unslinging his backpack from his shoulder, he reached inside for a bottle of water and tossed it to Rusty. "It isn't beer, but it'll keep you hydrated."

"Thanks." Rusty uncapped it, then took a long swig and closed is eyes. "Much better."

Callie watched the exchange, noting that Harlan seemed to be doing his best to avoid talking to her. Unable to take it any longer, she said, "So you ready to tell me yet?"

Now came the innocent look. "Tell you what?"

"What's been eating you all morning."

He faltered. "Is it that obvious?"

She glanced at Rusty, then took hold of Harlan's arm and pulled him closer to the hillside. "I haven't forgotten how to read you, Harlan. I know when something's up."

"I guess you would, considering we used to be connected at the hip. Although I'd think you'd be a little out of practice after all these years."

"Like riding a bicycle, I guess. Or a horse." She thought about her aching butt and wondered if there was a suitable analogy there. "So are you gonna tell me, or keep avoiding the question?"

"You may not want to hear it."

She frowned. "Why do you say that?"

"Because it's about you."

She hesitated, but now she was *really* curious. "A statement like that certainly won't discourage me," she said. "So you might as well spill."

Harlan looked down at his boots now, as if what he was about to say was both embarrassing and a little perplexing. Then he said, "I had a dream about you. About us. So real I could've sworn it was actually happening. That's why I was so flustered when you woke me this morning."

She narrowed her eyes at him. She thought she knew where this was headed, but wanted to make sure. "What kind of dream?"

"The kind of dream you don't want me having anymore. You came to me on the sofa wearing that oversize UC sweatshirt you always used to—"

"All right," Callie said. "I think I get it."

"That makes at least one of us."

"What do you mean?"

"I thought I was past all that. Yet here we are, together for less than twenty-four hours, and I'm already having dreams about you. I think that says something, don't you?"

Callie was surprised to discover that her heart had kicked up a notch. She tried to shrug it off. "Like what? That you're a man?"

"Come on, Callie, this isn't about sex and you know it."

"Oh? Then what's it about?"

"Forget it," he said. "I shouldn't have told you."

Too late, she thought, as a bucketful of images tumbled through her head—exactly the wrong *kind* of images. She was supposed to be focusing on this manhunt and all she could see were Harlan's lips and tongue and hands and…

Not about sex, huh? Then why couldn't she scrub these images from her brain? Now the damage was done and she realized her legs were trembling again. Only it had nothing to do with the long ride.

Calm yourself, Callie. For all your talk of forgiving and forgetting, this isn't really what you want. You've moved on. So stay moved on.

But had she? Really?

And if Harlan was having dreams like this, maybe *he* hadn't, either. Maybe they should both be paying close attention here.

But no, there was always that one thing that came between them. That one wedge that she just couldn't seem to shake loose.

Treacher.

Poor dead Treacher.

And the thought of him and everything that had happened that night always had an instant sobering effect on her. Instead of seeing *Harlan's* lips and tongue now, she saw Nicole Bittenger's lips and tongue, doing unspeakable things to Harlan. It was a part of this whole sordid mess she hadn't thought about in a long, long time, but she knew it was the glue that kept that wedge firmly in place.

Harlan had been with someone else when Treacher was killed.

He had always denied that anything had happened that night, but Callie hadn't been able to allow herself to believe him. To trust him. And if you can't trust the man you love, what's the point?

"I think you're right," she said. "You shouldn't have told me. Some things should remain unspoken."

"That's always been the problem, hasn't it?"

"Meaning what?"

"After the accident we spent a lot of time shouting past each other, but we never really sat down and talked about it. About exactly what happened."

Callie hardened. "I know what happened."

"That's the thing, Cal, you *think* you do, you think you have it worked out exactly how it went down, but you never really listened to my side of the story. You pretended to, but you made up your mind about me before I even walked in the door."

"People have eyes, Harlan. They told me what they saw."

He shook his head. "They got it wrong. It was a party, remember? They were drunk and too busy dealing with their own B.S. to pay any attention to..."

He paused, his gaze suddenly shifting to a spot above her right shoulder. The eyes tightened slightly, then grew wider.

Callie wheeled her head around, looking up toward the rocky hillside. "What is it? What's wrong?"

"I thought I saw something move up there. Someone watching us."

Callie scanned the hillside, looking up toward an outcropping of rocks, using a cupped hand to shade her eyes against the sunlight. She stared intently at those rocks, but saw nothing unusual.

But before she could tell Harlan this, he suddenly grabbed her arm and shouted, "Look out!"

An explosion went off and dust billowed, chunks of the mountain breaking free, the entire hillside soon following, a tidal wave of rock and debris tumbling toward them.

The horses whinnied in terror and began to

scatter, the thunder of their hooves drowned out by the rumble of the falling rock.

Harlan jerked on Callie's arm, pulling her out of the path of a rolling boulder.

"Go! Go!" he shouted, and the two kicked into motion, trying to avoid the onslaught.

She heard Mercer cry out in alarm and saw Rusty scramble to his feet as another boulder blasted past the deputy, coming within inches of flattening him.

They all ran, giving it everything they had, as the landslide bore down on them, the rocks and dirt seeming to consume them.

Harlan picked up speed, dragging Callie along with him as she saw Rusty go down, followed by Mercer. She let out a shrill, terrified shriek—

And before she knew it, her world was nothing but broken earth and stone as the avalanche pulled her and Harlan under.

Then everything was still.

Chapter Fifteen

When Harlan awoke, he was buried beneath the debris. He didn't know how much time had passed, but guessed it was seconds rather than minutes.

He tried to move. No pain. Didn't seem to be hurt in any substantial way. A gap in the rubble was letting air come through, and he could see daylight.

He still had hold of Callie's arm and could feel her pulse throbbing beneath his fingers.

Alive, thank God.

But in what condition?

"Callie?"

Nothing.

Releasing her, he twisted his body, shifting the earth around him until he was able to move his arms. He began pushing rocks and dirt aside and finally broke through to the surface.

"Callie?"

She uttered a faint, muffled groan.

Sounded far away.

His heart pounding, Harlan got to his feet and frantically burrowed through the mound of dirt and rock, tossing it in all directions until he finally found her—still in one piece, but rattled and a little banged up.

Her breaths came in long gulps as she drew in precious air. "...thank you..."

"Are you okay?" he asked. "Anything broken?"

She checked for any serious damage, then shook her head. "I... I—I don't think so."

Harlan pushed aside the rest of the debris and helped her to her feet. He heard more groans nearby and saw both Mercer and Rusty struggling to free themselves as well.

The way that hillside had come down, it was a miracle they were all alive.

"Everyone okay?" he asked.

Mercer grunted in the affirmative as he kicked some rubble aside and stood up, cursing under his breath.

Rusty said, "I think I may have twisted something, but I'll live. How are *you* guys?"

"Mad as hell," Callie said, still breathing hard. She rubbed her elbow as she wheeled around to look up at the mountain. "Who *was* that up there?"

Mercer cursed again, spitting dirt. "Our fugitives, is my guess. At least one of them. Must've come back to see if anyone was looking for 'em."

But Harlan wasn't so sure. "That sounded like a dynamite blast. Where would they get dynamite?"

"From Jonah, no doubt. Old guy was crazy enough to keep some handy. Maybe up at the cabin."

"Does that mean we're getting close?" Callie asked.

"According to Landry's map, we've still got the Lost Woods ahead of us." He gestured. "And I hope one of you still has a copy of the thing, because both it and my GPS are buried somewhere under this slide. I was checking our route when the blast went off."

Harlan climbed up and over the rubble toward the mountain, straining to see if anyone was still up there.

No sign of life.

"Whoever it was, I'm betting they're long gone. Probably started riding the minute they set off the blast."

"He better hope I don't catch him," Mercer said. "It won't be pretty if I do."

Callie looked concerned. "We've lost the element of surprise. What if they take off before we can get to them?"

Mercer dismissed the idea with a wave of the hand. "They take off, where they gonna go? This isn't exactly friendly country, and there aren't any more outlaw hideouts to head for. Besides, whoever did this thinks we're dead. *I* sure would."

"Maybe so," Harlan said, "but we need to move faster. No more rest stops."

The comment must have reminded Mercer about the horses. Looking visibly worried, he scanned the landscape until he found all four of them grazing a couple hundred yards away at the bottom of sloping incline. They looked unfazed now, as if the world hadn't just fallen apart around them.

Mercer let out a breath and said, "Gotta love those gals. Always sticking close to papa. More than I can say for my ex." He looked at the others. "I assume you folks are ready to mount up and go?"

Rusty was checking his right ankle. "Sooner I get off this thing, the better. Looks like it's starting to swell."

"All right, then," Mercer said, then put his fingers to his mouth and whistled. The horses responded immediately, coming toward them in a loping gallop.

Mercer dipped into his shirt pocket and found a wooden matchstick. Stuck it between his lips.

"Let's get after these cowards before they figure out we're still alive."

THERE'S NOTHING LIKE a brush with death to help you get your priorities straight.

As they continued along the overgrown trail, Callie realized that all this drama between her and Harlan was little more than trivial nonsense.

What did any of it matter right now?

What she needed to do was concentrate on the task at hand. Get the job done and worry about the rest after the killers were behind bars.

But even as she told herself this, she had to admit that when she'd heard Harlan's voice calling to her from beyond the rubble, the relief she'd felt had been palpable.

She thought for sure he hadn't survived the slide, and she couldn't quite fathom a world without him in it. She may not have seen him for a decade, but at least she had always known that he was out there somewhere. Living and breathing. Being Harlan.

And that meant a lot to her.

More than she was willing to say.

When she thought about it, she realized she had been just as happy to see him emerge from that burning house with Gloria Pritchard clinging to him. Even at the height of her anger toward him, that sudden fear of losing him had ripped through her like a dark tide.

If that meant she was still in love with him, then so be it. But she couldn't let it interfere with what they'd come here to do.

No distractions.

She needed to get down to business, and Harlan seemed to be feeling the same way. He had gotten quiet again as they rode along the trail, the Lost Woods looming up ahead. He had taken the lead now, using Landry's map to guide them, and his focus and stolid determination was a comfort to her.

It was also, she was beginning to realize, an aphrodisiac.

Why was she letting him get to her like this?

Concentrate, Callie.

No more personal drama.

THERE WERE A LOT OF LEGENDS surrounding the Lost Woods.

Several acres deep, it was a nearly impenetrable maze of ancient Douglas fir that stretched into the sky above them, their high, thick branches exposing only patches of blue. It was said to be haunted by the ghosts of outlaws past, men who had fled here to escape a posse only to find themselves hopelessly lost, and dead within days.

Except for the Pritchard gang, of course.

Others said that the trees themselves would watch whoever entered these woods, tripping them up with their gnarled roots, covering them with branches after they fell, so that their decaying bodies would become part of the earth and never be found.

Callie didn't take much stock in these legends. She wasn't the superstitious sort. But the moment they rode into the woods, the world seemed to grow darker—not simply the blocking of the sun by the trees, but a kind of kinetic darkness that swirled around them like the souls of angry spirits.

"Lovely place," Rusty said. "Tell me again why I volunteered for this manhunt?"

Mercer huffed a chuckle. "Who says you volunteered?"

"At least tell me I'm getting hazard pay. Somewhere there's gotta be a silver lining to this operation."

"The silver lining is waiting at that cabin," Callie told him. "When we catch the bad guys."

"Spoken like a true training deputy."

She knew he was only half-serious, but he was starting to grate. "And you're talking like a whiny rookie."

"Hey, what do you want from me? I almost got killed back there and my ankle hurts."

"So do my elbow and my butt," Callie said, "but you don't hear me complaining. At least we're still alive."

"And I'd like to stay that way, thank you very much."

She looked at him. "What are you trying to tell us, deputy? You don't think you're cut out for this job?"

"Just blowing off steam," he said.

"Well, blow it another direction. And be grateful we're still in one piece, even if your ankle *does* hurt."

She knew she sounded harsh, but she couldn't help herself. Maybe she needed to blow off a little steam, too.

She softened. "Look, Rusty, I'm sorry, but

this isn't much fun for any of us. Once we've got these creeps in jail, we can all go to the Oak Pit and get drunk. I'll even get that cop groupie with the fake boobs to massage your ankle if you want."

Rusty smiled. "You wouldn't have to try too hard. In fact, if the Pritchard Ranch hadn't burned up last night, I think I might've sealed the deal."

Uh-oh. TMI. She was suddenly sorry she'd brought up the subject. "Well, if you do get lucky, I hope you'll keep it to yourself."

His smile widened. "Don't worry, I'll try to limit it to just a few hundred of my friends."

Despite her mood, Callie managed a laugh. Rusty may have been a complainer, and he may have had trouble handling crime scenes, but he wasn't shy and he knew how to make her smile. He was a nice distraction from the gloom surrounding them.

When it came down to it, he was also a good cop. But as his training deputy, she was required to keep that tidbit of information to herself. She needed to help him build his confidence, not his ego.

Up ahead Harlan brought his horse to a

halt in the middle of a small clearing and signaled to the others to stop.

"What is it?" Callie asked.

He scanned the woods as they all pulled up alongside him. "Trail ended. No sign of it anywhere."

Callie looked back the way they'd come. The trail had indeed stopped at the edge of the clearing and didn't seem to pick up anywhere else.

"What does the map say?"

"That we follow it through the trees, and when we come through to the other side, we'll be just above Robbers Canyon."

A small spike of concern stuttered through Callie. "So where is it, then? Did we go off course?"

"Not according to Landry."

"Maybe he lied," Mercer said. "Another reason for refusing to come with us." He paused. "Ladies and gentlemen, I think we've officially been punked."

"But why?" Callie asked. "He's just set himself up for an obstruction charge. He could go to jail."

"You think so? He'll just claim he got it wrong, or he forgot. That we were pressuring him too much." Mercer swore under his breath.

"Or maybe he doesn't care," Harlan said. "Maybe he was setting *us* up at the get-go."

"How so?"

"What if that landslide wasn't caused by Billy Boy and his friends at all? What if the one we have to watch for is—"

A shot rang out, echoing in the trees. Mercer grunted and flew off his horse, landing hard on the ground, blood pumping from his upper left arm.

Harlan whipped around. "Down! Everybody down!"

Another shot rang out and they all dove, the bullet striking a nearby tree, splintering wood. One of the horses spooked and reared up, nearly stomping Mercer's head as her hooves came crashing down. Then it and the others scattered, galloping off into the trees.

More shots followed, one after another, the bullets punching the ground around them. Callie grabbed for her service weapon, but it was hard to tell what direction the shots were coming from, and she was too far away for her weapon to be effective. Unfortunately, their rifles were with the horses.

"Callie!" Harlan shouted. "Over here!"

She wheeled around and saw him dragging Mercer behind a tree. There was a momentary pause, then the shots started again as Callie and Rusty followed Harlan and dove for safety. They quickly pulled themselves upright, putting their backs to the tree, Rusty in pain, holding his ankle.

Her heart pounding wildly, Callie peered out into the woods but saw nothing. She glanced at Harlan and Mercer. Harlan had a hand clamped over the wound in Mercer's arm, trying to stop the flow of blood.

"How bad is it?"

"Not good," he said.

"I'm fine," Mercer grunted between gritted teeth, his face about three shades paler than usual. "Give me a gun. I'm gonna shoot this son of a—"

"Quiet," Harlan told him, then cocked his head to listen.

Silence.

The shots had stopped.

He gestured to Callie. "Keep your hand clamped over the wound. I'm going after this guy."

"What? How can you even tell where he is?"

"I'm guessing he's on the move, either getting out of here while the getting's good or looking for a better angle. Either way he's bound to make some noise."

She didn't like the idea of Harlan going out there alone. "Why don't we all just stay right here. Safety in numbers."

"And let him get away? Or worse yet, get into position and take us down? I don't think so." He gestured to the wound. "Take over."

Callie knew she couldn't stop Harlan, and arguing about it would only waste precious time. When he released the pressure, Mercer groaned. Callie quickly took Harlan's place, clamping her hand over the wound.

"See if you can stop the flow," he said. "If he loses too much blood, he's gone."

Callie nodded, then immediately reached down and unbuckled Mercer's belt. She'd have to use it as a tourniquet.

"Good thinking," Harlan said, then got to his feet and disappeared into the trees.

Chapter Sixteen

Harlan had never been in the military, but he was lucky enough to have military training of a sort. When he was nineteen, he and his big brother Sam had gone to a three-week boot camp in Montana where they'd learned the same tactical and evasive maneuvers that were taught in the marines. Not quite the same thing, sure, but it had given him a confidence that would have been sorely lacking otherwise.

After he was recruited by the feds, he'd trained at Glynco and found that much of that training was similar. And in his time with the Marshals Service he'd been in his share of tight situations, including a hostage recovery that had nearly gotten him killed.

In other words, Harlan was no stranger to violence. He may not have encountered it on a day-to-day basis, but he'd seen enough to know how to maintain calm and to focus on his objective: finding the shooter.

He had no doubt that it was Landry out here. The bogus map had sealed that conclusion. And judging by the way Bickham had been so quick to defend Jonah Pritchard yesterday afternoon, to confront three officers of the law with a shotgun, it was obvious where his loyalties lay. Baked-in loyalties, so to speak, and Harlan didn't think Jonah's death had changed anything. Despite what Meg Pritchard may or may not have done to her grandfather, Landry's mission was to protect and defend the family, and he was doing just that.

Harlan moved from tree to tree as quietly as possible, stopping to listen for any telltale sounds—the rustle of bushes, the scattering of birds, the crack of timber.

But he got nothing.

He was almost certain that the shots had come from this direction, but the more time he spent out here, the more he began to wonder if Landry had fled. The man wasn't exactly a young buck, and he had to know that any physical confrontation would only end with him getting hurt.

Harlan was starting to think this was an

exercise in futility, when he saw something out of the corner of his eye. Nothing more than a distant glint of light in the trees but it was enough to make him swivel his head and take a closer look.

And sure enough he saw it again, coming from higher ground, inside a clump of bushes. Light reflecting off a mirrored surface of some kind.

Or maybe the glass of a rifle scope?

If so, the shooter was about three hundred yards away up a slight incline, getting a bead on Callie and the others where they hid behind the trunk of that Douglas fir.

Knowing the shots would start up again soon, Harlan didn't waste any time. He began working his way again from tree to tree, moving as quickly and as stealthily as possible, circling around and behind the shooter's position.

Then taking his Glock from its holster, he crouched low and started inching toward that bush.

But as he got closer, his intuition kicked in and he suddenly realized that he was wrong. The shooter wasn't hiding inside that bush, and the light he'd seen was, in fact, nothing more than a mirror.

A decoy.

And as this realization set in, Harlan felt cold steel on the back of his head for the second time in forty-eight hours.

The barrel of a rifle.

"You'll want to drop that weapon, son."

Harlan cursed inwardly. Landry Bickham was behind him. And Harlan couldn't quite believe that he'd been duped twice in a row. All that training and what had it gotten him? He'd once again let his guard down in a tight situation and that wasn't good. It wasn't good at all.

What the heck was wrong with him?

"You're making a huge mistake here, Landry."

"Oh? How you figure? You folks'll be dead, I'll be alive and Meg and her friends will be able to ride out of here without you people interfering."

"I don't get it. Why are you helping them?"

"I don't see as how that's any of your business."

"Call me curious," Harlan said.

He honestly didn't care about Landry's motives, but he figured the longer he kept the man talking, the longer it would take him to pull the trigger.

"Well, you know what they say about curiosity," Landry told him. "And it looks as if it's about to come true for you."

So much for that plan.

Harlan heard the faint rustle of fabric and felt movement behind him and knew it was now or never. Shooting a hand back, he grabbed hold of the rifle barrel and twisted, just as the shot went off. The sound of the blast exploded against his right eardrum, pain piercing it as he turned, swung out hard and landed a solid blow to the center of Landry's face, using his Glock as a club.

Bickham shrieked and dropped the rifle as he stumbled back, grabbing at his broken nose, blood pouring between his fingers, his eyes wide with surprise and sudden horror.

Harlan kicked the rifle aside, then raised the Glock and trained it on him, saying, "One more move and I'll consider it an excuse to shoot you."

But the only move Landry Bickham had left in him was to drop to the ground, sitting in the dirt as he nursed his bleeding nose.

CALLIE SAID, "THERE'S NO POINT in holding out on us, Landry. We're gonna find out one way or another."

Harlan was having trouble hearing from his right ear. It had begun to ring, as if he had just come from a sound barrier-busting rock concert, and he wondered if it would ever go away.

Small price to pay for being alive, he supposed, but he'd much prefer to avoid having to wear a hearing aid for the rest of his life, if that was even remotely possible.

Once he'd gotten Landry back on his feet, he had cuffed his hands behind him and escorted the old fool back through the woods to where Callie and the others were situated. Callie had succeeded in stopping the flow of blood from Mercer's arm and he was already sitting upright, his face no longer looking quite as pale as it had been a few minutes ago.

Not that he was the picture of health. They all knew they had to get him to a hospital. And soon.

As Rusty hobbled through the woods trying to rustle up the horses—and a much-needed first aid kit in one of the saddle-bags—Callie took charge of questioning Bickham.

"You hear me, Landry? You might as well fess up."

"He broke my nose," Bickham said, a nasally twang to his voice.

"And you tried to kill us. Twice. So pardon me if I don't have a whole lot of sympathy for you."

"Shoulda done it back in that library. Taken that floozy of a librarian down with you."

Callie sighed. "Your not winning any friends here, Landry. You might want to consider being a little more cooperative before one of us hauls off and breaks that nose again."

Landry visibly winced. "I want a lawyer."

"You what?"

"A lawyer. I don't have to say nothin' without one. I know you think I'm stupid—most everyone does—but I got enough smarts to know my rights."

Harlan was a big believer in due process. More than once Callie had accused him of being a cowboy, but he had never been one of those law enforcement types who abused his power in the name of the greater good. He usually played it aboveboard and straight down the line. Collected his evidence the hard way, through good solid police work.

But to his mind today was different. This

man had nearly killed them more than once. Had dedicated himself to the task. Not only that, the people he was protecting had torched a vehicle with a man still inside and had done the same to a house after shooting two people. Not to mention they'd started this little crime spree with a fairly solid knock to the side of Harlan's head.

So seeing as how they were out in the middle of nowhere, and about as far from a lawyer as you could get without stepping foot on the moon, he didn't figure the due process really applied right now.

Sometimes a man had to do what a man had to do.

He and Callie exchanged looks, then Harlan said, "Cal, maybe you should see if you can help Rusty round up the horses."

"I'm fine," she told him.

Harlan shook his head. "No, we're talking plausible deniability here. The less eyes see what's about to happen, the better chance we have of Landry's complaint against us not holding up in court."

"What's about to happen?" Landry asked, fear now etching his face.

"Shut up, I'm not talking to you." He looked

at Callie again. "I mean it. Mr. Bickham and I need to have a private talk."

Callie didn't budge. "What about Sheriff Mercer?"

"In his condition I figure he's got built-in deniability."

Callie considered this a moment, and he could see the conflict in her eyes. He was half convinced she wouldn't go along, but then she said, "You know what?"

"What?"

"I think I just heard Rusty calling. Sounds like he needs my help."

Harlan nodded grimly. "Then I guess you'd better get moving."

They exchanged another look, and he could see the reluctance in her eyes, knew she wasn't completely in love with this plan of attack, but then she was gone and Harlan returned his attention to Landry.

"You touch me, you'll regret it," Bickham said. It was an empty threat and he knew it.

Harlan didn't respond with words. He casually reached forward and pinched Landry's nose between his first and middle fingers. He squeezed and Landry howled, dropping to his knees, tears popping into his eyes.

"Now, Landry, I couldn't care less about the reason you're here. I figure in that dim little brain of yours there's some kind of motivation at work, but I'll leave that for the forensic psychologists to decipher, assuming you're still alive when we're done."

Landry burbled something unintelligible but Harlan ignored him.

"Now we can take you back to town and get you a lawyer and hope that lawyer will convince you to make a deal with us and tell us what we want to know. But I've been riding a horse all day long and dodging rocks and bullets, and I didn't go through all that just to have to drag your sorry butt back home on the slim chance that you'll cooperate. Especially when one of those bullets has put a man I've come to respect in very serious danger."

Landry was moving his head around now, trying to break Harlan's grip, but Harlan and his brother Sam had seen their share of Three Stooges movies and he'd had a lot of practice with the old knuckle pinch. And judging by the look on Landry's face, fighting it was only making it hurt worse.

After a moment he gave up, now squeezing his eyes shut against what Harlan had to think was pretty unbearable pain.

"So here's what you're gonna do. From here on out, you're gonna shut your mouth unless I ask you a question. And if I ask you one, you'll answer me sincerely and without hesitation. You got that?"

Landry tried to nod his head.

"I'm glad we understand each other," Harlan said, then released him. Landry collapsed to the ground, trying desperately to recover, fresh blood staining his upper lip.

Harlan couldn't help feeling a little bad about it. Under normal circumstances he wasn't prone to violence, and he wasn't particularly proud of what he'd just done. But these weren't normal circumstances and considering what they'd been through, he figured his actions were more than justified.

"You listening to me, Landry?"

"Yes," the old fool croaked.

"Good," Harlan said. "I want to you to lie there for a while, start feeling better. And once we've got the sheriff here squared away for travel, I'm gonna send him and Rusty and Callie on their way. Then you and I are gonna go visit that cabin. No more phony maps. No more ambushes. You understand?"

"Yes," Landry croaked. "I understand."

Harlan showed him a slow smile.

"I figured you would."

Chapter Seventeen

Callie wasn't having any of it.

"No," she said, adamantly. "I'm not leaving. Not now."

They had found Landry's horse tied to a tree several yards from the spot where Harlan had snuck up on him. Harlan had uncuffed him just long enough to get him aboard, then snapped one cuff to the saddle horn and the other to his wrist.

In the meantime Rusty and Callie had rounded up their own horses, found Harlan's first aid kit and tended to Mercer's wound before getting him ready for travel.

Now Harlan was insisting that Callie go with Mercer and Rusty and leave him behind to deal with Landry and the fugitives.

"That's just not gonna happen," she told him.

"You trust Rusty to get the sheriff back in one piece?"

"He can get him within cell phone range. After that he'll call the medevac crew."

Callie wasn't about to let Harlan shove her aside. Not now. She'd already gone along with his blatant disregard for due process and didn't feel particularly good about it, even if it *had* resulted in Landry's full cooperation. To her mind such behavior was a slippery slope, and she could only hope that this had been an exception rather than the rule.

Harlan said, "Considering the amount of time we've wasted, it could be dark before we get to the hideout. I don't think this is a place you want to be after sundown."

"You're not changing my mind, Harlan. This is *my* investigation and I plan on seeing it through."

"It could get ugly."

"It already has," she said. "And in case you haven't noticed, I've managed to survive so far."

Harlan studied her for a moment, and a smile grew on his face.

"What are you grinning about?"

"To be perfectly honest," he said, "I was hoping you'd fight me on this."

"Oh? Why?"

"Despite our bickering, Cal, I kinda like

working with you." He sobered slightly. "I'm full of all kinds of regret, and I really wish it could've been this way all along. Lived that dream we always talked about. With or without Treacher."

Callie saw the sincerity in his expression. Knew the words were heartfelt. Tears unexpectedly threatened to fill her eyes, but she struggled to hold them back. She didn't want anyone here seeing her cry.

Especially Landry.

But in that moment whatever animosity she'd felt toward Harlan dissolved. Disappeared. She didn't know how long it would last, but it felt good to be free of it—even if only for a moment.

"So do I," she said softy. "So do I."

IT TOOK ANOTHER twenty minutes to get Rusty and Mercer on their way. Mercer's bandage was bloody, but with the tourniquet still in place, the flow seemed to have stopped for now and he assured them he had enough strength to see himself through to the nearest cell zone. That he could even sit atop his horse in his condition was a testament to his iron will.

"You be good to my gals," he said, struggling with his pain. "They get hurt, there'll be hell to pay."

Callie assured him they would, then watched the two men ride away, hoping against hope that they'd get the sheriff to safety before that wound started to bleed again.

When they were gone, Harlan and Callie mounted their own horses, then Harlan turned to Landry. "Showtime, Bickham. You plan on keeping your promise, or do you need a little reminder?"

Landry's eyes widened slightly, his free hand moving involuntarily toward his nose, as if to protect it. Then he caught himself and scowled. "You better hope nothing goes wrong out there, son. If it does, you're the first one on my list."

"Yeah? How's that working out for you so far?"

"Mark my words. You're a dead man."

Harlan's eyes glazed. "You know how many times I've been told that over the course of my career? I've transported men who'd make you pee your pants if you spent more than five minutes with them. So don't for a second think you can intimidate me, Bickham. If anyone should worry about winding up dead, it's you. I won't hesitate to shoot you, if I have to."

Landry had lived nearly his entire life with the Pritchards, and some of their arrogance had obviously rubbed off on him.

"You're good when a man's hands are cuffed," he said. "But that bruise on your face tells a different story."

Callie cut in. "You know what, Landry?"

He turned, scowled at her. "What?"

"I think I like it better when you smile."

"I'll bet you do," he said. "Everybody does."

He let one spread across his face now, but it was so full of malice that the hairs on the back of her neck prickled.

"Even your mother liked it," he said quietly. "Did I ever tell you I knew her in high school?"

Callie stiffened. "Not that I remember."

"Knew your daddy, too. Even before I started workin' for the Pritchards. He and Mary were quite the couple. But old Jonah, well, he just couldn't abide by some tramp corrupting his perfect little son."

"Call her that again," Callie said, "and I'll shoot you myself."

Landry shrugged. "It's not like I'm the

first one to say it. But I never felt any ill will toward her. Truth is, I had a crush on her. If things had been different, who knows? You might be calling *me* daddy."

The thought made Callie want to puke. But then it occurred to her that Landry was only trying to get a rise out of her. Keep her off guard and eventually he might be able to use her discomfort to make a move. She wasn't sure how he'd do it with his hand cuffed to the saddle, but there was no point in taking chances, and she refused to let him get to her.

"Nice try," she said. "But my mother wouldn't have come anywhere near you even if she was dying of thirst and you had a bucketful of water."

"Just shows how little you know. I'll bet that grandma of yours painted a nice little picture."

"I think you need to shut up now."

"You're completely clueless, aren't you?"

"Enough, Bickham," Harlan barked. "Don't make me pull you down off that horse."

Landry swiveled his head toward Harlan. "Hold on, now, I think this girl deserves to know about her family. About her momma *and* her daddy." He returned his attention to Callie. "You probably believe all that nonsense about Riley Pritchard getting himself killed in a truck accident."

"It's the truth."

Landry chuckled. "The truth can be manufactured if you've got enough money. We all learn that every time we turn on the TV. But I know the *real* truth about your daddy, and if you want me to keep it to myself, I'll respect your wishes. Let you go on believing in fairy tales."

Something sour turned in Callie's stomach. She knew he was still playing with her, baiting her, but she also felt compelled to listen. Nana had never told her a whole lot about what had happened to her father, and she wondered if Landry really *did* know something.

"Tell me," she said.

His smile widened, and she wondered why she had never noticed the ugliness behind it. "You sure you want to hear this?"

"Tell me," she said again.

Harlan had good enough sense to stay quiet now. He would instinctively want to protect her, but he knew by the tone of her voice that this wasn't the time to interfere.

Landry said, "Like I told you, your daddy didn't die in no truck accident."

"How, then?"

He waited a moment for dramatic effect. "Boy up and killed himself. Slit his wrists, right there in his barracks."

Callie's stomach flip-flopped and she felt prickles on her scalp. Could this be true?

"How do you know that?"

"Everybody in the Pritchard family knows it."

"I don't understand. Why? Why would he do that? Because his father forced him to join the army?"

"Jonah didn't force him to do nothin'. He cherished that boy. Riley decided to run off on his own. When he found out about Mary."

"Because she was pregnant?"

Landry huffed. "No, he was over the moon about that. You could barely contain the boy. He was gonna be a *father*."

Callie was at a loss. "Then why? Why would he run away?"

"Because six months into her pregnancy, Mary told him the truth."

"About what?"

"That he wasn't your daddy after all. Turns out Mary wasn't a one-man kinda gal."

Callie's gut tightend and he held her gaze, his eyes burning with intensity. He was enjoying this. And despite her skepticism, she had to ask the question.

"Let's assume for a minute that you aren't a lying sack of garbage. If Riley didn't get my mother pregnant, who did?"

Landry showed her his most malevolent smile yet.

"Why, Jonah Pritchard, that's who."

Chapter Eighteen

The world turned sideways.

Callie felt a rush of dizziness slam into her and she nearly fell out of the saddle. She really *was* going to be sick now. Could feel the bile rising in her throat.

She didn't think she'd ever come this close to fainting before, even when she got the news about Treacher. But she was close now. Had to muster up every bit of her will to keep from diving headfirst into the dirt.

Sensing her distress, Harlan nudged his horse up alongside hers and grabbed hold of her arm. "You okay?"

She was trying to control her breathing. Couldn't get enough air to form any words.

"How you expect the girl to be okay?" Landry said. "News like that is bound to trouble *anyone.*"

"Shut up, Bickham," Harlan snapped.

"I'm just the messenger. She's the one insisted I tell her."

"I said, shut up. You say another word, I'll pull you off of that horse and beat you to a pulp. You understand?"

"Whatever you say, Marshal."

Harlan glared at him then returned his attention to Callie. The world was starting to right itself now, and she was finally able to breathe.

"Easy, Cal. Just take it slow…"

She knew he must be thinking he'd walked straight into one of Nana Jean's soap operas, but his blue eyes showed nothing but concern and she was grateful for that.

"I'm good," she said. "Thank you."

At least she hoped she was.

The thought that her mother had ever gone near Jonah Pritchard's bed was ridiculous.

Wasn't it?

He squeezed her arm. "Take your time."

She put her hand on his and squeezed back. "No, I'm okay now. I'm fine."

"Well, ain't you two love birds a picture?" Landry said. "Just like Jonah and Mary. Of course, she was a good thirty years younger than him."

Harlan turned, sitting upright in his saddle.

"Your nose looks like it stopped bleeding, Bickham. You want me to fix that for you?"

"Anybody ever tell you you're a violent man?"

"I'm not the one running around trying to kill people, remember? Keep flapping your gums and you'll find out what violence really is."

Landry opened his mouth, then immediately closed it again, finally smart enough to heed Harlan's warning.

Something else that Callie was grateful for.

There was no way to know if he was telling the truth about her mother and Jonah, and she could only hope that he was the lying sack she thought he was. But Gloria's unspoken accusation kept tumbling through her head, and that was enough to stir up some doubt.

Of course her mother had been eighteen at the time of her pregnancy, and was known to be a bit of a wild child. Was it possible that she had been attracted to Jonah? Had she been dating Riley, but secretly sleeping with his old man?

The thought sickened Callie, but then that's exactly what it was designed to do.

Landry was playing mind games. Trying to exploit a weakness where he saw it, to gain some kind of leverage over her.

But it wouldn't work unless she let it.

And she wasn't about to let it.

She steeled herself and sat upright, refusing to give in to his emotional terrorism.

"Can we get moving now?" she said to Harlan. "The sooner this creep and his friends are behind bars, the better I'll feel."

ONCE THEY GOT STARTED, they rode for another hour, continuing to wind their way through the Lost Woods. They had picked up the trail again, right where Landry had promised it would be, so at least he wasn't taking them on a wild goose chase.

Or so they hoped.

They still had no idea why he'd gone to so much trouble to help a trio of unapologetic sociopaths. It seemed odd to Callie that his loyalty was so strong that he was willing to kill for them—especially after they'd shot Jonah—but she had long ago given up on trying to figure out what motivates criminal behavior. People killed for the stupidest reasons, so in a perverse kind of way, maybe Landry was to be commended. At least he hadn't gutted anyone over a pair of tennis shoes.

Not that this would make Sheriff Mercer feel any better. And Callie doubted it would color a jury's verdict once she testified against the old fool. But on the list of motives for attempted murder, loyalty wouldn't even be close to the top.

Landry obviously felt that someone he cared about was being threatened, and had decided to do something about it. And back in the outlaw days he probably would've had a lot of townsfolk cheering him on, just as they'd cheered on Jeremiah Pritchard.

But the outlaw days were over. Even out here in the middle of nowhere.

Maybe someone had forgotten to tell Landry.

The sun was almost gone by the time they reached the far side of the woods and found themselves on a high bluff overlooking a canyon.

Calling it a canyon was being generous. It was really little more than a crevice in the earth, the mountains on either side rising toward the sky like protective walls shielding it from any but the most observant eyes.

No helicopter would be able to find it. And

it was no wonder that none of the posses of the past had ever made it this far.

"Robbers Canyon," Landry said, then gestured to the lip of the bluff where a narrow trail snaked treacherously into the crevice. "It's getting dark. Might want to postpone the rest of this trip 'til daylight."

"How long is the ride?" Harlan asked.

"Ten, fifteen minutes, I'd guess. Never really timed it."

"And what are we walking into when we get down there?"

"Another trail. Five-minute ride around a couple outcroppings before we hit the cabin."

Callie could see the wariness on Harlan's face. They had no real reason to believe this man, and every reason to assume he was sending them straight into an ambush.

Landry sensed Harlan's hesitation. "What's the matter, Marshal? Don't you trust me?"

"We trusted you to draw us a map," Harlan said. "And look where that got us."

"That was before you so kindly reminded me how much I value my life." He gestured to his nose. "And my extremities."

"Doesn't help that you threaten to kill

us every chance you get. And tried a few times."

"All true, but you're a man and you know how it is. Gotta put up a good front, make sure your opponent knows you ain't no push-over. Especially in front of a lady. But after this long ride, I've seen the error of my ways."

"Not if you think I swallowed a single word you just said."

Landry snorted. "Good one. I like that." He looked out at the sky. "But the more we jaw, the closer it gets to sundown. So what's it gonna be, Marshal? Yay or nay?"

Harlan looked down at the canyon, then up again at Callie. "What do you think, Cal? Think we should trust this creep?"

"We don't have much choice. It's about the only thing we *can* do at this point."

"Now you see there? That's a smart girl," Landry said. "It's all that Pritchard blood running through her. Even if it is watered down a bit."

Callie swiveled her head. "You're gonna want to knock that off right now."

"You know, you remind me of your mother. She and I used to smoke cigarettes back of the band building at school. Did a little necking now and then, too, although I never did get past second base with her."

Now Harlan chimed in. "Stow it, Bickham."

But Landry wasn't listening. "One day she up and tells me all about her little love affair with Jonah Pritchard. Says he may be older, but he's the kindest, most giving lover she's ever—"

"All right," Callie said, turning to Harlan. "Either we tie this weasel to a tree and leave him up here, or I'm gonna be forced to use my firearm."

"I opt for the firearm," Harlan said, and he didn't sound as if he was joking.

Landry took a look at their faces. "Now wait just a minute."

"What do you say we let fate decide?" Callie said, then climbed off her horse and gestured. "If I find rope in this saddlebag, then that's that. But if it's empty, I'll take that as a sign I need to empty my gun, too."

Harlan nodded. "Works for me."

"Now hold on," Landry said, his gaze going straight to the saddlebag. "This ain't funny. You want me to shut up, I'll shut up. I was just havin' a laugh."

"Too late," Harlan said. "You played your last card and it was a joker."

Callie reached for the saddlebag in question and unfastened the flap. Flipping it open, she shoved a hand inside and pulled out a coil of rope.

"Lucky you," she said. "I guess that joker was wild."

Landry's entire body went slack. He looked relieved but defeated. She was pleased to see that all the fight had drained out of him.

Of course she'd *known* there would be rope inside. She had put it there before they'd left Pritchard Ranch, and Harlan had seen her do it. But if Landry could mess with people's heads, so could she. And she almost felt ashamed by the amount of pleasure it had given her.

Almost.

"Tree it is," she said, then hefted the rope. "Although this might make a pretty good noose."

Harlan nodded again. "That works, too."

"You people are just flat-out cruel and sadistic."

Callie smiled. "That's not it at all, Landry. We just don't like you."

Five minutes later they had him cuffed,

gagged and tied to a tree, with a promise that they'd do their best not to forget about him.

The look on Landry's face was one that Callie knew she would cherish for many years to come.

Chapter Nineteen

They decided to enter the canyon on foot.

Despite the growing darkness they knew that their horses were a visual target, and if anyone should be waiting for them, the potential of being spotted was much too high.

Besides, navigating such a treacherous trail in the dark on horseback wasn't exactly a wise move. As much as Callie loved the animals, she figured there was less risk of taking a tumble if she was traveling on her own two feet.

The trail was narrow enough that looking down into the canyon made her heart pound a little. It was a long drop, and a simple misstep could end in disaster.

She and Harlan moved quickly but carefully, using flashlights, but only turning them on when they absolutely had to. It wouldn't do to have Billy Boy or Meg or

Creep Number Three see bobbing lights on the mountainside and sound the alarm.

Callie said, "We better hope Landry doesn't get loose up there."

"Are you kidding me? He'd need the intervention of the Almighty to do it. And I'd rather risk that than risk him giving us away."

"I was just making noise, but I have to tell you, a part of me really did want to shoot him."

"I don't blame you," Harlan said, "all that garbage he was spewing about your mother?"

"You think he was telling the truth?"

"Based on what little I know about Landry Bickham, I'd say that he and the truth have been strangers for a very long time."

"Maybe so, but he sure got me wondering."

"Tell me this," Harlan said. "Does it really make a difference? Father, grandfather, either way Jonah Pritchard is dead, and when he was alive he didn't want to have anything to do with you. If it were me, I'd wash my hands of the whole thing."

"I keep thinking about my mother. Nana Jean has always painted this rosy picture of her and if she had anything to do with Riley killing himself—"

"You'll tie yourself up in knots if you start thinking like that." He took hold of her wrist and they stopped. "But maybe there's a lesson in this. One we can both benefit from."

"What do you mean?" Callie asked.

"Maybe we shouldn't be so quick to believe what people tell us. They embellish, they exaggerate and sometimes they flat-out lie. And everything is filtered through their own experiences, their own prejudices."

"Why do I get the feeling this isn't about my mother?"

"Because you aren't a stupid woman," Harlan said. "I know this isn't the time to be getting into this, but once we're done here, I'd like you to do me a favor."

"And what's that?"

"I'd like you to sit down with me and let me tell you what happened the night Treacher died. Treacher getting drunk, Nicole, the whole nine yards. And I'm talking about the truth, not a bunch of so-called eyewitness accounts by people who could barely stand up straight."

Callie instantly felt the walls going up—

the way they always did when she was confronted by that night. But when she thought about all the shouting and the crying that she and Harlan had done in the aftermath, all the accusations, she realized she never really *had* given him his say. Not without a knee-jerk reaction to every other word he spoke.

She had closed him out without apology. She knew that now, and there was no excuse for it. She'd paid dearly these past ten years because of it.

It occurred to her that being so deeply in love with someone was a double-edged sword. There was the joy, the exhilaration, but there was also the fear, the insecurity, the jealousy and anger—all of which stemmed not from the relationship itself, but from a personal lack of self-confidence. The inability to believe that someone can love as much as he is loved back.

The key, she realized, was trust and communication. Listen to each other and don't jump to conclusions, no matter what someone outside that relationship might say.

Callie knew she owed Harlan his chance to explain. And even if that explanation didn't live up to scrutiny, at least she could take comfort in knowing that she'd been *fair* with him. This time.

As they stood there in the middle of that narrow trail, Harlan's hand on her wrist, the darkness gathered around them, she reached up with her free hand and touched his jaw, then leaned forward and kissed his cheek.

"It's the least I can do," she said.

Then he turned his head toward her, put his mouth on hers and gave her a real kiss, before moving past her and continuing on down the trail.

And as Callie watched him, she once again thought about her trembling thighs and knew that what she felt in them had nothing to do with the ride.

LANDRY BICKHAM COULDN'T help laughing.

All his life everyone had looked at him as dumb old Landry, the boy who never could. There may have been some truth to that in school where he'd always had trouble paying attention, but for every ounce of book learning he lacked, he'd earned a pound of street smarts. And he knew a man couldn't get through this life without a fair bit of improvisation.

As incongruous as it might seem—considering he was a sunbaked old ranch hand—unlike Jonah, Landry had never been a big fan of outlaws. Landry's hero, believe or not, was a little Hungarian-born fella called Eric Weisz, otherwise known as Harry Houdini.

If you were to sift through the rubble of the Pritchard home and work your way down to the basement where Landry kept a bedroom, you'd find the charred remains of his Houdini collection. Half a dozen biographies, several how-to books, and even a couple of old silent movies the magician had made to capitalize on his popularity.

It killed Landry to know they were all gone now, but such is life, and they'd be easy enough to replace.

Landry had performed a few card tricks in his time, but he'd never found much fun in it. Oh, he could hold his own in the sleight-of-hand department, but it didn't interest him all that much, unless he could find a way to get something out of it.

His true skill had always been knowing how to read people. To figure out how to manipulate and misdirect them, just like any good magician. He may not have been big on fancy card moves, but he could win a pot with a smile and a wink, or get a woman to lie down with him with a few simple words, or make a self-possessed old coot like Jonah Pritchard think he was running the show.

It sometimes took a fair amount of improvisation, but like Harry Houdini, Landry was good on his feet. He could control a conversation and make a couple of lightweights like Callie Glass and U.S. Deputy Marshal Cole react pretty much the way he wanted them, too.

Once they'd caught him in the woods, he'd known full well that if he pushed them hard enough, they would do exactly what they'd done. Leave him alone up here while they went off to perform their so-called duty. Such as it was.

He had gotten a kick out watching little Callie play her game with him. She was a tough gal when she needed to be—everybody knew that—but she'd never been the type to up and shoot someone just because he'd rattled her cage a bit. It had been fun watching her, however, and he felt a tiny chuckle coming on just thinking about it.

Misdirection and manipulation. Controlling the dialogue and knowing how to get people looking at your left hand when they should be watching the right. Which is why, as Marshal Cole slapped these cuffs on one wrist, Landry was busy using his free hand to pick the Marshal's pocket.

Quickly, deftly and accurately.

And by the time the cuffs were snapped shut behind him, Landry had clipped the key between his fingers in a way that would make his hands look empty. It was a trick old Harry used to do before they locked him in a trunk and dumped him in the river. Or turned him upside down and stuck him in a tank full of water.

Ropes and knots had never been a challenge for Landry, so once the cuffs were off, everything else was gravy. And five minutes after they'd left him behind, he was on his feet and headed for the trail.

People might think he was dumb, all right…

But he was nobody's fool.

THEY SMELLED BURNING WOOD long before they reached the cabin.

They were close to the second outcropping when smoke wafted in their direction, and Harlan help up a hand, signaling for Callie to stop. Crouching low, he moved to the tip of the outcropping and peeked over the edge of the largest stone.

Callie moved up next to him. With the darkness came the cold, and she could feel it seeping in through the fabric of her jacket. They stayed close, sharing their warmth.

There was a clearing ahead, the cabin sitting about three hundred yards away, looking almost exactly as it had in the archive photo but larger than she had expected. The only thing missing was a desperado staring intently into the camera.

Without cell phone reception or electricity, Callie felt as if she had been thrown into the past, to a simpler, more primitive time. It was the same feeling she'd gotten as a child, when she and Nana Jean had visited a ghost town near Parkerville which had remained untouched since its abandonment a century before.

A saloon. A blacksmith's shop. A general store. A large old mansion that the tour guide had referred to as a "house of ill repute"— which, to nine-year-old Callie, had sounded like a hospital of some kind.

Like that old town, there was calmness to the air here. A peace. And she suddenly understood why Jonah liked coming here.

"Someone's home," Harlan whispered.

A kerosene lamp hung from a hook in the

front window, its yellow light flickering. They watched intently for a moment, then saw movement in the light. A shadow passing through it.

"There's bound to be a back way in," Callie said, then looked at the mountain walls surrounding the clearing. There was some exposure here and there, but plenty of cover, too, which would allow her to work her way around to the rear of the cabin. "Give me about three minutes."

She was about to go when Harlan stopped her.

"No," he said, "Let me do it."

She shook her head. "You're too big of a target."

"And if they spot you, they won't hesitate to shoot you. I won't have that on my conscience."

Callie frowned. "We're both professionals, Harlan. I can handle myself. And since I'm probably half your size, there's less chance they'll spot me."

She could see from his expression that he knew she was right, even if he didn't like the idea. She heard the reluctance in his voice.

"Three minutes," he told her. "Then I'm going in."

"I'll be there."

"You get yourself shot, I'll never forgive you."

"If I get myself shot, don't expect me to be as stoic as Mercer. I'll be crying like a baby."

"All the more reason not to," he said.

She grinned at him, then climbed down from the outcropping. Staying low, she carefully edged her way past it, keeping her eyes on the cabin as she darted across a narrow stretch of the clearing to a cluster of rocks on the other side.

She hunkered down behind them, eyeing that flickering light, looking for any sign of life in the window. Satisfied that no one was watching her, she stood up again and made another dash, moving laterally toward another group of rocks.

From here she knew it was just a matter of climbing up a small, rocky hillside and around to the rear of the cabin.

Checking the window again, she made her way up and over the rocks and began to climb, moving as quickly as she could, leaping from stone to stone and hoping she wasn't making too much noise.

Less than a minute later she stood in a cluster of trees, looking down at the rear of the cabin. It seemed much bigger up close, with at least two or three bedrooms. There was another window back here, and she knew if she could get close enough, she'd be able see inside.

Checking for signs of movement, she moved into a crouch and slowly worked her way down the hillside until she was only feet from the cabin. She heard voices inside, angry voices, but the sound was muffled, and there was no way for her to identify them.

She made a last quick dash now and was directly below the window. The voices were louder, more distinct. Steeling herself, Callie slowly edged her head up past the window sill and peered inside.

What she saw froze her to the spot.

There were two men and woman in the room. Megan, of course, sitting in a chair by the fire, rocking back and forth like a little kid who had just been severely traumatized and was trying to block out the world.

One of the men was pacing, a kid of about twenty-two or so, the kid from Harlan's surveillance photos—Billy Boy Lyman. The other man was seated at a table, Billy Boy waving the business end of a shotgun at the back of his head. But he wasn't the one called Brett, and Callie couldn't quite fathom what she was seeing here. It put the lie to everything she'd believed about this case since yesterday afternoon.

"Come on, you old fart, I'm losing my patience. Sign the paper and I'll kill you fast. Otherwise you're gonna think I'm the devil himself."

The man in the chair said nothing. Didn't move. Just looked defiantly at Billy Boy.

Which didn't surprise Callie in the least.

The old man in the chair was none other than Jonah Pritchard.

Chapter Twenty

Billy Boy was becoming more and more restless. This wasn't going at all the way he had hoped it would.

Meg had promised him that the old man would cave the minute Billy threatened to kill her. Said he had a soft spot for her. All Billy had to do was play his part, and Pritchard would give them anything they wanted.

Unfortunately Meg had underestimated her influence over the old man. Turned out he wasn't so anxious to be cooperative after all.

Their plan, such as it was, had been hatched days ago, back when Billy first got the news that the judge in Colorado Springs had decided to ship him up to Torrington while he was waiting for trial. This was shortly after he got tagged for the bank robbery—another one of Meg's brilliant ideas—and Meg and Brett came to visit him at county.

"We're gonna bust you out," she told him. A proclamation that Billy had greeted with some very sincere skepticism.

Meg Pritchard was one of hottest women he'd ever known. Wore that body of hers like it was some kind of weapon, and she was an expert marksman, that was for sure. Shortly after he met her, however—and boy did he remember *that* night—Billy had to admit to himself that not only did Meg have a crazy streak, but was probably not the brightest planetary star in the galactic empire.

The idea of actually breaking someone out of jail sounded like something you'd see on a television show, but Meg was so freaking lovely to look at you couldn't help but give her a listen, even if what she was saying didn't make a whole lot of sense.

"And how do you plan on pulling off this big escape?" he asked. They were sitting across from each other in the visiting room and the guard on duty had made Meg put on an oversize T-shirt for fear that what she was wearing would rile up the inmates. Billy didn't doubt that it would.

"Easy," she told him. "When they transport you up to Torrington, they'll have to take the main highway, right?"

Billy nodded. "I guess so. Most direct route."

"Well, there's a stretch along there that's deader than the moon. Only thing around for miles is this little gas station mini-mart place, stays open twenty-four hours."

"So?"

"So that's where we do it. You pretend you've gotta use the facilities, and we'll be there waiting for you the minute you step foot in that store. Bing, bang, boom, you're free."

Bing, bang, boom, huh?

Billy thought about this genius plan, and knew there were just too many things that could go wrong. "What if the guy doing the transporting don't wanna stop?"

"You'll just have to convince him. Keep talking to him the whole ride, try to get on his nerves. Trust me, he'll be happy for the break."

Billy's skepticism hadn't waned. "I don't know. Sounds pretty dumb to me."

This was when Meg had started to pout. She always looked cute when she did it, but

Billy hated it. She'd get all grouchy and start holding out on him and eventually he'd have to give in to her anyway.

He looked at Brett, who had been sitting there silently the whole time. Probably because he was twice as dumb as Meg. They'd all met in juvie a few years back and had been friends ever since.

Billy said, "What do *you* think of this idea?"

Brett shrugged. "Could work, I guess."

That was about as much of a commitment he'd ever get out of the guy, and Billy figured it was enough. Besides, what did he really have to lose?

"All right," he said to Meg. "Let's do it."

Even if it hadn't worked out, the expression on her face had been enough of a reward. Lord, she was hot. If this lame-brained plan had even half a chance of getting him close to what was under that T-shirt again, it was well worth the effort.

And surprise, surprise, Meg had turned out to be right.

The problems started when Billy found out the rest of the plan. This didn't happen until they'd knocked the Marshal out and hit the road in Brett's Malibu. Brett was driving while Meg and Billy got frisky in the backseat—no T-shirts this time—and man oh man, she was looking better than ever.

When they were done, Billy wanted to know where they were headed, where they'd hide, and Meg informed him that they were going to her grandfather's house.

"Now why would we want to do that?" Billy asked.

"Two reasons," she said. "He worships me and he's the guardian of my trust fund."

This was news to Billy. "Trust fund?"

"Fifteen million dollars. Enough money to get us out of the country and then some. Maybe head to Barcelona. I always wanted to go to Italy." Then she offered him a smile so dazzling he had to plant a kiss on those ripe red lips of hers. Of course the sudden revelation that she was the richest woman he'd ever met might have had something to do with it.

Question was, if she had all this money waiting for her, why on earth had she convinced him and Brett to rob a freaking bank?

This chick really *was* crazy.

"So what does this mean, your gramps being guardian of the fund?"

"Means I can't get the money without his signature."

"Will he sign it over?"

"Hah," she said. "Not likely. Not without a little convincing."

"You said he worships you."

"Which is why he won't sign. Figures it's in my best interest to make me wait until I'm thirty before I can collect it."

"Thirty? What's the point of that? Half your life is over."

"Tell me about it," Meg said.

"So how do you plan on convincing him to sign?"

She smiled again, as if what she was about to reveal was the most brilliant scheme any human being on the planet had ever come up with.

"Piece of pie with chocolate ice cream," she said. "We make him think you're gonna hurt me if he doesn't."

Now this was when Billy realized he had a major problem on his hands. Because this was, without a doubt, even dumber than her plan to help him escape. Except *that* plan had managed to work out just fine.

So should he be listening carefully now?

"We show up at the ranch," she told him.

"Introduce you as a couple friends of mine. So far so good. Only once we're inside, we make it clear to the old coot that I'm actually your hostage and unless gramps does what you tell him to do, you'll waste me right there in front of him."

"Doesn't making him sign the money over to you kinda give you away?"

"Who cares, as long as I got my money? Besides, it won't much matter at that point."

"Why?" Billy asked.

"Why you think?" she said. "We're gonna kill him."

Billy considered this, and the thought of fifteen million bucks might have been clouding his judgment a bit. "And you really think this is gonna work?"

"He's got all the paperwork right there in his study. He'll sign it in a heartbeat if he thinks he's gonna lose his precious little Megs."

Billy wasn't convinced. "This is a working ranch, right?"

"Right."

"And you expect me and Brett to waltz in there and start threatening you when he's surrounded by all these people who work for him? I can imagine some of those ranch hands are pretty tough."

"Nothing to worry about," she said.

"How you figure?"

"I've got a man on the inside. He'll make sure the place is cleared out shortly after we get there. He's Grandpa's right-hand man and pretty much runs the show around there."

"Man on the inside," Billy said suspiciously. "This isn't some guy you're sleeping with, is it?"

Meg scrunched her nose at him. "Ew, give me some credit, Billy. He's my real father. Only nobody knows I know that."

"Real father? I thought your parents were divorced. Wasn't your daddy some guy named Breen?"

"Yeah, except he was just a friend of Grandpa's. He was only pretending to be my father because Grandpa didn't want anyone knowing my real dad was some lowlife ranch hand."

What the heck?

"You got one seriously screwed up family, you know that?"

"Tell me about it."

"So if your real dad is such a lowlife, how come gramps keeps him around?"

"What can I say," Meg told him with a shrug. "Everybody loves Landry."

EVERYBODY LOVES LANDRY, huh? Everybody but Billy, maybe. When they showed up at the ranch, he'd taken an instant dislike to the man. Didn't like the way the guy kept sizing him up as if he was trying to decide whether or not Billy was good enough for Meg—which was a laugh considering how seriously twisted everyone on Pritchard Planet was.

Whatever the case, Megan's plan turned out to be just as worthless as Billy had suspected it was. Old man Pritchard wasn't buying any of it, not from the get-go, and before they knew it a couple of sheriffs showed up towing none other than Marshal Harlan Cole along with them.

All because Meg had gotten the bright idea to hijack a truck, then rob the guy and torch him on the highway.

To Billy's surprise, however, Pritchard covered for them. Then after the cops left, all hell broke loose in the Pritchard mansion and poor Brett wound up dead.

Seemed Landry had some kind of lame-brained scheme of his own, which included double-crossing Meg, Billy and even

Grandpa Moneybags with that shotgun he was holding. Maybe he figured he'd just kill everybody, starting with Brett, then blame it on Meg and Billy and pocket that Pritchard money for himself.

How exactly that was supposed to work was beyond Billy's ability to reason, but there it was, a complete mess by any definition. And in all the confusion, Meg and Billy just barely managed to grab some horses and get the heck out of Dodge, taking Grandpa along with them before this Landry fool shot them all.

Now here they were in some remote freaking cabin—Meg's idea again—trying to get Grandpa to cooperate and sign the papers she'd stolen from his safe. But Grandpa was no pushover. Grandpa was probably one of the orneriest, most infuriating people Billy Boy had ever had to deal with.

"Come on, Pritchard, you're what? Eighty-three years old?"

Pritchard said nothing.

"What've you got to live for anyway? Even your own granddaughter wants you dead."

He glanced over at Meg, who had been sitting by the fireplace for a good hour, her head in her hands as she rocked back and forth in her chair. The closer they'd gotten to this place, the more subdued she'd become, as if some very bad memories were coming back to her, and she couldn't quite handle the weight.

Pritchard finally broke his silence. "You don't know what you're talking about," he said. "Megan loves me."

"If you believe that, pops, you are one deluded old cowboy."

"She loves me and she knows it. Always has, always will. Isn't that right, Meg?"

Meg didn't respond to him. Just kept rocking. Billy was really starting to get worried about her.

Pritchard looked at him intently now. "Even if I do sign this paper, it won't mean a thing. You and Meg are wanted by the law. What makes you think she'd even have a chance to get to these funds?"

"What are you talking about? They're hers, ain't they?"

"I always knew that girl wasn't college material, but I never figured she'd hook up with somebody quite as idiotic as you."

All right, Billy thought. That was enough. He ratcheted the shotgun and pressed the barrel to the back of Pritchard's head. "Last chance, gramps. Sign it or die."

"Is that what you want, Megan? You want him to shoot me? You know how much I love you. I've showed you that every chance I got. I've always been your sweet Grandpa J, remember?"

Billy expected Meg to go on rocking, but she surprised him when she suddenly stopped. She looked up at Pritchard, and there was pain in her eyes like he'd never seen before. Like the eyes of a puppy who's been tortured and can't quite figure why.

But there was also heat there. Anger. "My sweet Grandpa J?" she said. "My sweet Grandpa J?"

"Remember you used to call me that when I tucked you into bed at night?"

Billy watched as Meg's face went though half a dozen different emotions before settling on what he could only describe as pure, unadulterated rage.

She jumped to her feet, her face beet red, shouting, *"My sweet Grandpa J?"* Then she looked at Billy like a rabid skunk and said, "Shoot him, Billy!"

Billy took a small step backward. "What?"

"I don't care if he signs the paper. Just shoot him. Pull that trigger and shoot him!"

"What about the money?"

She took a step toward them now. "Did you hear what I just told you? I don't *care* about the money. It's dirty money anyway. A payoff for his guilty conscience. He's a sick, disgusting old man. So just shoot him now, before I take that shotgun and do it myself."

That was when the door to the bedroom flew open and the lady sheriff pointed a gun at Billy.

"Drop the weapon right now, Lyman, or the only one who gets shot is you."

Chapter Twenty-One

Billy Boy didn't drop the shotgun. Not right away. And Callie was starting to wonder if he ever would.

She was also starting to wonder where Harlan was. He should've been here by now. She'd waited as long as she could outside the back window, before circling around to one of the bedrooms and climbing in, knowing the closed door would give her cover.

She'd stood next to the door, listening to the two men long enough to get a broad idea of what Billy Boy was up to, and it still hadn't made a whole lot of sense. And since she hadn't seen their friend Brett in the room, she'd assumed that it was *his* body burnt to a crisp back at the Pritchard Ranch. Which meant both Landry and Gloria had lied.

But why? To protect Meg?

If so, then why had Gloria claimed Meg was the one who had pulled the trigger?

Try as she might, Callie hadn't been able to figure it out. And all she'd wanted was to get this whole sordid affair over and done with. Get all these idiots squared away and dumped in a jail cell where they belonged, and let some other poor fool sort through the mess.

Then she could go home, see how Nana Jean was doing and finally sit down with Harlan—where the heck *was* he?—to listen to what he had to say.

That wasn't too much to ask, was it?

But with Megan screaming for Lyman to pull the trigger, Callie had figured she had only seconds to act, so, Harlan or no Harlan, she'd done what she had to do. She'd burst into the room, trained her Glock on Billy Boy and hoped and prayed he had enough brains to be cooperative.

"I mean it, Lyman, drop the weapon. *Now.*"

For a moment there, Callie thought everything would be all right. From the look in Billy Boy's eyes he seemed to know that this was a done deal, that he might as well give it up and take his chances with a jury. And old Jonah looked relieved, even thankful.

But now Meg was shouting even louder, nearly frothing at the mouth. "Don't listen to her, Billy! Shoot him. Shoot that old monster!"

And when Callie told her to shut up and sit back down, Meg scowled at her and charged, coming at her like a ball of intense white heat.

Callie had no choice but to turn the Glock on her and fire. She aimed for the calf, hit a solid piece of flesh and Meg went down to the floor hard, howling in agony.

But apparently this was a deal breaker, because now Billy Boy swung around in a rage and pointed the shotgun at Callie. "What'd you go and do *that* for?"

He was at such close range that the blast would cut her right in two, and as his finger wrapped around the trigger, she went into a dive.

Suddenly Jonah Pritchard leapt out of the chair and tackled the kid, knocking him to floor.

The shotgun went off, shattering a window, and now Jonah was straddling Billy, starting to pound the living daylights out of him. Hitting his head and face over and over again.

Callie rolled and got to her feet and pointed the Glock at them, "Enough!" she shouted. "That's enough, Jonah! I think he got the message."

Jonah stopped and nodded, Billy Boy bleeding and barely able to move, but alive and breathing.

As Callie kicked the shotgun aside, Jonah got to his feet and went to Meg, crouching down to check her wounded leg. The moment he touched her, however, she jerked away from him. "Leave me alone, you creep!"

Jonah said, "I don't know what your mother told you, girl, I don't know how she managed to poison your mind, but I've never laid a finger on you."

"I know what you did," she cried. "I remember it."

"I don't see how that's possible, because it never happened. Not once. Not ever. I'd kill myself before I'd hurt you."

Jonah seemed quite adamant about this and Callie didn't know what to make of him. Was he telling the truth? Had Gloria implanted false memories in Meg's brain just to get her daughter hating a father she'd long resented?

If so, it had to be one the cruelest forms of child abuse Callie had ever encountered.

Jonah untucked his shirt tails and tore off a strip of fabric, tying it around Meg's leg to stem the bleeding. Then he picked her up and took her over to the sofa near the fireplace and laid her down.

He looked up at Callie. "She's losing blood. We need to get her to a hospital."

He was right, of course, but this wasn't Callie's first concern. She was worried about Harlan. Even after the shotgun blast, he hadn't made an appearance.

So where was he?

The question was answered a split second later as the cabin door burst open.

Landry Bickham stood in the doorway, smiling that Landry smile, a big black gun in his hand pointed directly at Callie.

"Nice to see you again, Cal." He tossed some rope to the middle of the room. "Now it's *your* turn to get tied up."

CALLIE WAS AT A LOSS. How could Landry have gotten loose? He'd been cuffed and hog-tied to a tree.

Her heart was beating uncontrollably. And not in a good way. "Where's Marshal Cole?" she asked him.

Landry gestured. "Back there in the dark, taking a little nap."

"Is he alive?"

"I hit him pretty hard," Landry said. "Woulda shot him, too, but I didn't want to attract any attention."

Callie felt sick. Felt tears dampening her eyes. "You son of a—"

"Now, now, Cal, if it makes you feel any better, you won't much care in a few minutes time." He gestured. "You might as well put that gun down. You won't be able to use it. Not before I use mine."

Callie wanted to smack that smile off his face. She hesitated, then crouched down and set her Glock on the floor.

"Now kick it over here," he said.

She did as she was told and he picked it up, stuffing it into his waistband. "Shotgun, too."

Callie stepped over to the shotgun and kicked it in his direction. He bent down and scooped it up, then tucked his gun away and ratcheted a round into the shotgun's chamber.

"Now I want you to take those ropes and tie Grandpa and his little love muffin up."

"And if I refuse?"

Landry pointed the shotgun at Billy Boy and pulled the trigger. Billy Boy immediately stopped moving.

And breathing.

Jonah, who was still crouched next to Meg on the sofa, visibly flinched and got to his feet again, staring at Landry in disbelief. "You just killed that boy in cold blood."

"Indeed I did." Landry looked at Callie. "That answer your question?"

His ability to shoot an unarmed man told her everything she needed to know about him. All this time she'd thought *Megan* was the sociopath. But looking at Bickham, she saw nothing behind his dark eyes but emptiness. The body he inhabited contained neither heart nor soul.

Jonah said, "Why are you doing this, Landry?"

"Does it really make a difference?"

"I think I have a right to know."

"A right?" Landry laughed. "Now that's just like you, isn't it, Jonah? You think you have a right to know and do and say just about anything you want. Because you have money. You're the big, rich man with all the privileges."

"You want some of that money? Is that it?"

"Honestly? I couldn't care less. I'm here for Gloria. She's tired of waiting around for you to kick the bucket."

"So that's it, is it? The two of you did this together?"

Landry laughed again. "As you well know, Jonah, this ain't the only thing the two of us did together. And I'm sorry to say that that mental case you're fawning over right now is the fruit of my loins."

"That's no way for a father to talk."

"Father? You never let me be a father to her. You were too ashamed to think some cowboy like me had soiled your bloodline." He gestured. "Callie here knows a little bit about that."

Jonah didn't respond and Callie said nothing.

"Gloria didn't want that little headache anymore than I did. You're the one insisted she be born. And now look what we've got—a murdering psychopath."

Apple doesn't fall too far from the tree, Callie thought.

"I don't get it," she said to Landry. "If you

haven't been trying to protect Meg all this time, what *have* you been up to?"

"Trying to finish what we started yesterday afternoon. Claim Gloria's inheritance."

"I don't understand."

"I can see where you'd be confused, all these people trying to muddy up the waters with their own idiotic agendas. But the truth is simple enough. Megan here contacted me and wanted me to help her get her boyfriend out of a jam. And Gloria and I knew this was our perfect opportunity to clean some house and lay the blame on Little Miss Nutbucket and her friends."

"How can you talk like that?" Jonah hissed. "She's your own daughter, for godsakes."

"Didn't we just cover that ground? Keep up, Jonah. Your last few minutes alive, I want you to understand just how much your *own* daughter hates you."

"I know I haven't been the perfect father."

"Perfect father?" He huffed a chuckle. "Ask Callie here something about that. You go and knock up her ma, barely eighteen years old, then pretend like she don't even exist. How far from perfect you think that qualifies for?"

The knot tightened in Callie's stomach but Jonah looked indignant. "Where did you hear that ludicrous story?"

"Where else? From Gloria."

Callie frowned. "You said my *mother* told you that."

Landry shrugged. "So maybe I embellished a little."

"Or a lot," Jonah said. "Don't believe a word of this, Callie. I never went near your mother."

"It don't make a whole lot of difference," Landry said. "In a few minutes you'll all be dead anyway, and Meg and her friends will take the blame so Gloria can collect her rightful inheritance."

"I don't get it," Callie said. "If Gloria's behind all this, how did she get shot?"

Landry smiled. "That was just our way of convincing you folks that our story was true. I gotta say I didn't want her going inside that burning house, but she's a brave little filly, and she figured that would seal the deal."

"Not to spoil your fun, but aren't you forgetting something?"

"And what would that be?"

"Sheriff Mercer and Deputy Wilcox. They

know you were the one trying to kill us in the woods."

Landry shrugged again. "They've got no proof Gloria had anything to do with it, and she's all I really care about. That's why I've stayed at Pritchard Ranch as long as I have." He smiled. "Besides, I was only trying to scare you folks off out of concern for Jonah. I knew these psychopaths had ahold of him, and didn't want your interference getting him killed."

"You think anyone will buy that nonsense?"

"You throw enough money at people, they'll buy anything. I may do a little time, but it's nothing I can't handle and Gloria will be waiting for me when I get out." His expression hardened and he gestured with the shotgun. "Enough chitchat. Show and tell is over. I think it's time you do what I told you and start tying these two up."

He stepped backward in the doorway, bent down and picked something up from the porch, then dropped it on the floor in front of her.

It was a large canister of kerosene.

"And when you're done," he said. "my little psychopath of a daughter is gonna start another fire."

Chapter Twenty-Two

When he came awake, Harlan smelled smoke.

His head was pounding, a sharp wet pain coming from the back of his cranium, the night air cutting into it like a rusty blade.

He groaned involuntarily, and a voice above him said, "So you're alive after all. Guess I didn't hit you hard enough."

Landry Bickham.

Hands grabbed Harlan's jacket collar and Bickham started dragging him through the dirt, the smoke swirling around them now, getting thicker with each step.

Harlan's world was spinning, nausea rolling through his stomach in waves. He wanted to fight back, but his strength had been drained by the blow, his muscles weak, his limbs refusing to cooperate.

Bickham kept dragging him, the dirt and rock cutting into his back, and Harlan twisted slightly trying to see where they were headed, wondering where Callie was, worried that she might be hurt.

Or worse.

He caught a glimpse of the cabin, smoke billowing out of its windows, and something thudded in his stomach. He didn't know what had happened here, but the fact that Bickham was still alive and on the loose was not a good sign.

"You must be wondering what you got yourself into, Marshal. We're working on a little weeny roast, and you're the weeny. But don't worry, I'll tell 'em how you managed to save me right before the place went up."

They approached the open doorway and Harlan knew this was his chance to make a move.

But could he do it? Did he have the strength?

There was only one way to find out.

As they passed through the doorway, Harlan felt the heat of the flames and willed his muscles into motion. Throwing his arms out, he grabbed hold of the doorframe with both hands, bringing Bickham to an abrupt halt.

Bickham stumbled slightly and released

Harlan's collar, and now Harlan twisted onto his stomach and lunged forward, grabbing Landry's leg.

Bickham cursed and tried to kick him loose, but Harlan hung on, pulling out and upward, sending Landry sprawling. He hit the floor with a thud, and it was only then that Harlan realized the entire interior of the cabin was ablaze, flames crawling up the walls toward the roof.

Harlan willed himself to his feet, the room spinning, the fire growing around him. But now Bickham was upright and fumbling for his gun, gripping it with both hands as he aimed it in Harlan's direction.

He fired and Harlan dropped to the ground again, narrowly avoiding the hit. Something cracked above him and a piece of the cabin wall came loose, splinters of fiery wood showering down toward him.

Harlan scrambled out of the way, and saw that Bickham was getting to his feet now, trying to clear smoke from his eyes as he pointed the barrel of the gun in Harlan's direction again.

The flames were growing in intensity and there was no place for Harlan to go. No way to avoid the shot.

But just as Landry was about to pull the trigger, there was another loud crack and a chunk of the roof caved in, a blackened, flaming beam of wood dropping down toward him. He snapped his head upward, saw what was coming and dove, but the edge of the beam caught his shoulder, knocking him forward.

He skidded across the floor, flames jutting up from the back of his jacket. He screamed in horror as he struggled to pull it off, then suddenly, another beam fell, the roof crashing down on him, the flames consuming him like a ravenous beast.

Harlan watched it all in a kind of stunned slow motion, but he didn't waste any time mourning the man's death. He knew that Callie and the others had to be in this cabin somewhere and he needed to get to them, fast.

Climbing to his feet again, he spun around and saw two doors, one of them already engulfed in flames. Fighting the smoke, he staggered to the door on his left, hoping and praying he had the right one. He pressed his hands against it, feeling for heat, then threw the door open.

He saw Callie cuffed to a bed post, her

terrified face lit up by the flames. And to his surprise, Jonah Pritchard and his granddaughter Megan were sitting on the floor next to her, both bound with ropes. Pritchard was coughing violently, choking on the smoke.

As the flames started to eat up the doorway behind him, Harlan crossed to them, surprise and relief in Callie's eyes.

"Thank God," she said. "Thank God you're alive."

"Are you hurt?"

She shook her head. "Just the smoke. You need to get Jonah out of here."

"First things first," he said, then grabbed hold of the cuffs with one hand as he reached into the watch pocket of his jeans with the other, fumbling for the key.

It wasn't there.

"The key," he said. "I don't have the key."

"Landry. He must have taken it from you. That's how he got loose."

Harlan yanked at the cuffs, but they were securely fastened to the wooden bed post, impossible to break. Jonah started coughing again and Callie gestured. "I'll be all right for a few minutes. You really need to get Meg and Jonah out of here."

"I'm not leaving you."

"I'll be fine. Just hurry."

The smoke was growing thicker. Harlan swiveled around and found the window, then crossed to it and shoved it open, smoke immediately swirling toward it as cool air rushed in. Returning to Jonah, he quickly untied his bonds then pulled the old man to his feet.

There was no time to untie Meg.

"I'll get your granddaughter," he said. "Wait outside the window."

Jonah stifled a cough and nodded, then hurried across the room and climbed through the window, turning back to wait for Harlan. Harlan scooped Megan up in his arms and she groaned, but offered little resistance as he carried her through the smoke and handed her off to Jonah.

"Can you handle her alone?" he asked.

Jonah coughed, nodded. "I think so."

"Get as far away from this place as you can," Harlan said, then took a gulp of the fresh air and turned around, swaying slightly, the pain from his head injury weakening his knees.

Fighting his way through the smoke, he crossed back to Callie who was coughing violently now, struggling to free herself from the cuffs.

"I can't get them loose," she gasped. "There's no way to do it. Just go, get out of here before this place comes down."

"Forget it," Harlan told her.

Stepping back, he raised his right foot and slammed the sole of his boot into the bedpost.

It splintered slightly, but held fast.

The flames were getting closer now, crawling up the walls of the bedroom, eating their way toward the roof, the heat nearly as stifling as the smoke.

His head swimming, sweat pouring, Harlan stepped back and raised his foot again, slamming it into the post.

More splinters, but still no joy. He'd been running on pure adrenalin and he was losing strength fast.

"Go!" Callie shouted, her gaze on the flames. "Get out before it's too late!"

But Harlan refused, again stepping back and raising his foot a third time, mustering all the strength he could manage. Then he slammed it home and the bed post finally gave, coming apart from the frame. He kicked it again and again, breaking it loose, the flames crawling across the floor toward them as Callie finally pulled the cuffs free.

Relief charging through them, they both stumbled to the window and dove through the opening, rolling onto the dirt outside. Then they were on their feet and running, getting as far away from the cabin as they could.

And as they collapsed to the ground, the flames consumed the old structure as what remained of the roof finally gave way, fiery timbers cracking and tumbling until the walls started to cave in.

They stared at it in stunned silence for a moment, then Harlan touched the back of his head, feeling the wetness there. Callie moved over to him and checked it.

"He got you pretty good," she said. "You're gonna need stitches."

"Doesn't matter," Harlan told her. "All I care about is that you're alive. I don't know how I would have functioned without you. I tried that and it didn't work."

She smiled now, leaning her head on his shoulder, tears filling her eyes, glistening in the flickering firelight.

"I love you, Harlan. I've never stopped loving you. Even when I hated you."

"I know," he said. "I know."

Then he pulled her close and kissed her forehead. Her nose. Her lips.

And all the evils of the world went far, far away.

Chapter Twenty-Three

It was up to Callie to go for help.

At daybreak she made her way up the trail and found Mercer's horses where they had left them, then rode for several hours until she was within cell phone range.

The rescue team came in helicopters, picking Callie up in a wide clearing, then following her directions until they found Robbers Canyon.

As Landry had warned, there was no real place to land, so the team was forced to hover above the canyon as rescuers made fast rope descends and hooked Megan, Jonah and Harlan into harnesses to pull them out of there.

Megan looked pale from the loss of blood, but Jonah's tourniquet had managed to stop the bleeding and the paramedics assured them that her prognosis was good.

"Until she comes to," Callie said to Harlan. "Then she'll probably wish she'd joined her boyfriend in the afterlife."

Harlan nodded. "I look at people like this and realize just how normal my life really is."

"You and me both," Callie said. "You and me both."

THE WOUND IN HARLAN'S HEAD took twenty-three stitches. The doctor warned him of a possible concussion, but his pupils seemed fine, and his only real concern was a throbbing headache that was expected to last for several hours.

Callie herself had a body full of cuts and bruises, but nothing serious enough to warrant more than some healing salve and a bandage or two.

The same couldn't be said for Sheriff Mercer, however, who had nearly lost his leg to an infection over the past twenty-four hours. Fortunately the doctors had managed to fight it off, and Mercer was expected to make a full recovery.

It turned out that Rusty Wilcox's ankle had suffered a full-fledged fracture and he wound up in a cast.

"Looks like you're off the hook for a while," he told Callie. "Won't be stuck training me."

"You've pretty much proven yourself, Deputy. But don't think this gets you out of any work. Cast or no cast, there'll be plenty of paperwork to deal with."

"Not as fun as dodging bullets," he said, "but right now paperwork sounds pretty darn good."

Gloria Pritchard was missing in action.

Shortly after Rusty and Mercer had been picked up by the medevac team the night before, word of Landry Bickham's rogue behavior had been delivered to their colleagues, and a couple of homicide deputies had gone to the hospital to question her.

She had answered calmly and politely, claiming to know nothing about what Landry might be up to. But within two hours of their departure, she had checked herself out of the hospital and left in a taxi.

She hadn't been seen since.

She wouldn't be getting any help from Jonah. Before Callie left Robbers Canyon to summon the rescue team, Pritchard had made it clear that he wanted nothing to do with his daughter, blaming her for everything, including all that was wrong with Megan.

"I don't understand that woman," he told them, his stoic pride still intact despite what had happened. "I've given her everything she ever wanted or needed. I can't believe she betrayed me like this."

There seemed, however, to be very little regret in his voice. Which, to Callie's mind, said a lot more about him than his words ever would. And blaming anyone but himself for the disaster his family had become was typical Jonah.

So now Gloria was on her own and would soon be struck from his will. She had once again failed to get what she had sought. She'd lost her youth, her looks and the Pritchard family fortune; all because of vanity and greed, and her stubborn refusal to allow time and fate to run their course.

She probably had a significant amount of cash stashed somewhere and had boarded a private plane shortly after she'd been questioned by the deputies. She must have assumed that Landry would be caught and would eventually give her up and was likely headed for Europe or South America.

Whether she had loved Landry or had

merely used him as a means to an end was something only she knew. But Callie suspected that Gloria had no more conscience than her daughter did, and Callie was surprised it had taken Gloria so long to finally act on her hatred for her father.

As Callie and Harlan left the hospital, she caught a glimpse of Jonah in the waiting room holding vigil for his beloved granddaughter. He had to know that his money couldn't buy her out of a murder charge, and that Megan felt no more love for him than Gloria had. Yet there he was, still clinging to the pathetic hope that he might somehow turn it all around.

Were the rumors about him true? Had he done to Megan what Gloria had accused him of? Or had a mother indeed brainwashed her daughter into believing the unspeakable had happened?

There was no way to know, of course, and Callie decided to set aside her own prejudices and give Jonah the benefit of the doubt. Maybe because a very small part of her felt sorry for him.

Somewhere in there, beneath the stony exterior, was a man who was now very much alone.

And Callie wouldn't wish that on anyone.

Nana Jean's tests showed that she was anemic, which explained her occasional dizzy spells. Judith had been kind enough to take her home from the hospital the previous afternoon, and had spent the night making sure there were no more mishaps and that Nana took her prescribed medication.

Nana was ecstatic when she finally got Callie's call.

"I was worried sick about you. When are you coming home?"

"Just as soon as we wrap things up here."

"Are you bringing you-know-who with you?"

Callie knew she shouldn't be surprised by the question. She sometimes thought Nana knew her better than she knew herself. "I haven't asked him."

"Child, don't you dare blow this opportunity. You lost him once, don't lose him again. He's a keeper."

"You don't even know him," Callie said.

"Don't need to. I see it in your eyes every time you talk about him. Even when you're angry with him."

Callie thought about this and had to laugh.

"You think you're pretty smart, don't you, Nana?"

"I just know what I know," she said.

WHEN HARLAN WAS DONE getting his head stitched up, Callie offered him another night's lodging.

She said, "I assume you don't have any objections."

"That sofa isn't the most comfortable thing I've ever slept on."

"Who says you'll be sleeping on the sofa? Someone has to keep an eye on you. Make sure you don't have a concussion."

He smiled. "In that case, how could I possibly refuse?"

It was well after sundown when they walked in the door to find Nana waiting for them in the parlor with a plate of sandwiches and a pitcher of iced tea.

After the hugs and kisses were over, she said to Harlan, "Glad to see you used your time wisely."

Harlan eyed her as if he'd just discovered that Nana was Wyoming's oldest and wisest sage. "You knew this would happen, didn't you?"

"I had a pretty good idea. I figured all you

two had to do was stop bumping heads and sooner or later you'd start bumping—"

"Okay, Nana, we get the picture," Callie told her, her face turning red.

Then they all started laughing and Callie and Harlan pulled up chairs and ate their sandwiches and drank their tea.

When they were done clearing the dishes, Nana disappeared into her room to get some rest, giving Callie a squeeze of the hand and a wink as she left. "You be sure to take care of that plumbing now."

When she was gone, Callie and Harlan went into the living room and Callie gestured to the sofa. "So that dream you had?"

"What about it?"

"What exactly were we doing that got you so hot and bothered?"

"I think it would be much easier to show you than tell you."

Then he kissed her, and she slipped her tongue between his lips as she ran her hands along his lower back.

She said, "What about your head?"

"What about it?"

"I wouldn't want to jangle anything loose up there."

"Damage is already done," he said. "I'm

crazy about you, Cal." Then he sighed. "I can't believe I let you go so easily. Instead of getting angry with you, I should have forced you to listen to me."

She kissed him again. "Let's forget about all that, okay?"

But he shook his head. "I don't want to spoil the mood, but we need to talk about it. The elephant in the room. If you want this to work, you need to hear my side of what happened to Treacher, once and for all."

Callie stiffened. "Can't it wait?"

"You know it can't."

He was right. But just the mere mention of that time made the walls go up.

She fought against those walls and nodded, then pulled away from him and sat on the sofa.

"All right," she said. "Tell me your story."

Chapter Twenty-Four

Harlan sat next to her, trying to find a way to ease into this without getting Callie's back up. But then he decided to just get on with it. No hedging. No sugarcoating.

"Treacher was stir-crazy that night," he said. "We'd all been studying so hard for finals and he insisted I go with him to the party. Tried to get you to go, too, remember?"

She nodded. "I remember."

"So we get there and the first thing he does is hit the cooler. Passes me a beer and tells me he's gonna circulate. I wasn't really in the mood, so I found a chair and kicked back, drank my beer." He looked at her. "And that was all I had to drink."

She nodded.

"So I'm sitting there doing the slow sip when Nicole Bittenger perches herself on the arm of the chair and starts talking to me. She was already three sheets to the wind, and I was worried she'd wind up flat on her face."

He saw Callie stiffen slightly. She had always believed the story circulated around campus that he and Nicole had hooked up that night, and all he could do was tell her the truth and hope for the best.

He said, "But that's *all* we did. Talk. Mostly about Treacher. Nicole was interested in him and wanted to know if I knew what Treacher thought of her."

Callie didn't look convinced. "And what did you tell her?"

"I told her I didn't know, but that Treacher was a straightforward guy and if she wanted to find out, all she had to do was ask." He paused. "You knew Nicole, so you can imagine how that worked out."

"She threw herself at him."

"In all her drunken glory. But by that time Treacher was pretty drunk himself and when I finally climbed out of my chair, I found them out on the back patio in the middle of a clinch, and it didn't look like either of them was ready to come up for air. But just as I was about to leave, Treacher saw me standing there and gave the look."

"The look?"

"The *get me out of here* look. As drunk as he was, he still seemed to have the presence of mind to know that getting involved with Nicole was a huge mistake. Yet here he was, making out with her."

"That isn't the way *I* heard it," Callie said. "People told me that you and Treacher got in a fight over her. That you were angry because he'd lured her away."

Harlan shook his head. "Not true at all. I just told him I wanted to go home and I thought he should, too, and I asked him for his keys so I could drive. He agreed and got to his feet, but Nicole didn't want him to leave and started getting upset. I tried to calm her down, but she was a pretty nasty drunk and things got ugly. We were alone out there, so I have to assume that people heard the yelling and thought it was Treacher and me going at each other with Nicole in the middle."

He could see that Callie was still on the fence. The old wounds were opening again. "So they were lying when they said they saw you take Nicole upstairs?"

He shook his head. "No. That much is true. She was in the middle of her tirade when all of sudden she said she was gonna be sick, so I told Treacher to stay put and rushed her upstairs to the bathroom." He paused. "I spent the next twenty minutes holding her hair as she leaned over the toilet bowl."

And paid dearly for his chivalry.

"You expect me to believe this?"

"I expect you to trust me, Cal. Did I ever give you reason not to?"

She hesitated. "No. I guess you didn't."

"When Nicole was done being sick, I cleaned her up, then took her into one of the bedrooms and laid her across the bed. But by the time I got back downstairs, Treacher was nowhere to be found. I checked the patio and every room of that house, then finally went outside and saw his car was gone. He'd left without me." Harlan looked at her. "And I haven't lived a day without wishing I'd ignored Nicole and just taken him home."

He waited as Callie processed the story. It was the truth—the truth he'd never had a chance to tell her after she'd been corrupted by rumors and vicious backbiting lies. But he had no way of knowing if she believed him now.

All he could do was hope.

Then her eyes filled with tears and she brought her hands to her face.

"Oh, my God," she said. "Oh, my God. I feel so…ashamed."

He ran a hand over her shoulder. "No. This isn't your fault."

"I should have listened to you."

"And I should have *made* you hear me. But neither of us was thinking rationally at the time. We'd just lost our best friend. We were upset and angry and too caught up in our own pain to realize what we were doing to each other."

"I'm no better than Jonah Pritchard," she said.

"What do you mean?"

"I let pride control me. Every time I thought about you, every time I wondered where you were or what you were up to, I let it keep me from contacting you. Maybe I *am* part of that family after all."

"Don't even think that, Cal. You're the exact opposite of what those people are."

"It's in my blood."

"Blood has nothing to do with it," he said. "All that matters is what's in here." He touched his chest, then touched hers. "Maybe you jumped to conclusions, maybe you believed what people told you, but you were broken and grieving and that can cloud anyone's judgment. But your heart is pure, Cal. Gentle. Kind. You would never purposely hurt another human being unless you were forced to."

"I hurt *you*," she said.

Harlan shook his head. "You went with what felt right at the time. We both did. And it was mistake. A terrible mistake." He cupped her chin. Tilted her head toward him. "But now we're free. No more walls between us."

Then he kissed her.

THEY MADE LOVE IN THE SHOWER.

Both of them had been anxious to wash away the past couple days, and the decade preceding them.

They undressed together in her bathroom, Callie staring at his body, marveling at how age had made him even more attractive. The wide, hard shoulders. The strong, workingman's arms. The ripple of his abs. And below…already showing signs of awakening as he pulled off her shirt, her jeans, her bra, her panties.

She felt her excitement build as she stared

at him, anticipating him inside her, remembering the exquisite pleasure they had shared so many times, so long ago.

Then they were beneath the water, its glorious warmth washing down over them as they lathered each other with soap. Harlan rubbed the bar between his palms, then ran his hands over her breasts, pausing to caress her hardened nipples, gently clipping them between his fingers, squeezing them.

Something loosened inside of Callie. Something wet and wonderful. And as the water washed away the suds, Harlan leaned forward and put his mouth where his hands had been, using his tongue and teeth to tease her.

All she could think about was feeling him inside her. Gently pushing him away, she turned her back to him and pressed up against him, feeling his hardness. The urgency of it.

Grabbing hold of him, she guided him forward and he brought his hands to her hips and thrust into her, grunting softly. He kissed her neck, her shoulders, and Callie felt heat rising inside her, tunneling its way toward her brain, causing tiny bursts of pleasure along the way.

Then his right hand moved forward, pressing against her pelvis as he thrust, and soon they were groaning in unison, working toward that place that seemed so hard to find with other men.

But Harlan wasn't just any man. He was her soul mate. Her true love. Her *only* love.

And as their duet of groans built to a crescendo, Callie felt her scalp start to prickle and thought for a moment that she might not survive the explosion inside her head. But then it came, wave after wave of intense pleasure causing her to cry out as Harlan went rigid against her.

But she suddenly realized that something was wrong. His reaction felt more like surprise than enjoyment. And as the last of the waves began to pass, he quickly pulled away from her, his hand gripping her arm.

Then a voice said, "Well, well, like mother like daughter. I guess skank runs in the family."

Dread sluiced through Callie's body as she whipped her head around to find the shower door hanging open.

Gloria Pritchard was pointing a gun at them.

Chapter Twenty-Five

"Come on, now, don't be shy," she said, gesturing with the gun. Her wounded thigh was stained with blood, but she didn't seem to feel it. "Callie, I need you to step out of that shower and get yourself dried off. We're going for a ride."

Callie was trying to cover herself with her hands. "What are you doing here, Gloria? What do you want?"

"To finish what I started thirty-four years ago." She gestured again. "Now get out and towel off." She pointed the gun toward Harlan. "And you stay put, Marshal. I've got no argument with you." She ran her gaze over his nakedness. "No argument at all."

Harlan started forward. "Don't be stupid, Ms. Pritchard. Put that thing down before you—"

The gun went off, the sound of the shot

reverberating against the walls as a hole opened up in the tile above Harlan's head.

Both Callie and Harlan flinched, ducking down involuntarily.

"You were saying, Marshal?"

Harlan didn't move.

Gloria pointed the gun at Callie. "You'd both better listen to me or the next one ends it right here and now."

"Ends what?" Callie asked. "Are you here because of Landry?"

Gloria laughed. "Oh, please, give me more credit than that. Now, hurry it up. I don't like to be kept waiting."

Callie's heart was pounding, but she did what she was told, grabbing a towel from the rack and quickly drying herself. Then she crossed to a hook on the wall next to the sink and took her robe down, slipping into it.

As she tied it at her waist, she said, "We thought you'd be long gone by now."

"So did I," Gloria said. "But when I started thinking about it, I knew I had some unfinished business before I left town. I was hoping Landry would take care of you out there in Robbers Canyon, but he blew it, as usual. I hope his last minutes were painful."

"You're sick," Callie said.

"Now you sound like my dear father. But you're right. I'm sick, he's sick, we're all sick. Every single one of us. Including you and your love toy here. All it takes are the right circumstances at the right time. But if you want to lay blame for this, point that finger at your little slut of a mother. She's the reason I'm here." She gestured with the gun again. "Now turn around and back toward me."

Again Callie did as she was told. "What does my mother have to do with any of this?"

"More than you could possibly know."

"I don't understand."

Gloria grabbed hold of Callie's waist tie and pulled her close, putting the gun to the side of Callie's head. "Marshal, I can see that look in your eyes, but if you try anything, the first bullet is for her, the second one for you. Then I'll go find her precious Nana Jean and put one in the old biddy while she sleeps."

"Ms. Pritchard," Harlan said. "Please. This isn't gonna get you anything. There's no upside here."

"I beg to differ, hot stuff. The upside is the satisfaction I'll feel when your little love muffin is finally dead."

Callie stiffened. "But why? What have I ever done to you?"

"What do you think, Callie? You were born, that's what."

Again Callie was at a loss.

"You don't get it, do you?" Gloria said, now backing her through the doorway into the bedroom. "The minute my father found out that my dear brother had gotten your mother pregnant, my entire world changed."

"But why? What did you have to with it?"

"Because it was *my fault,* don't you see? Your mother was my best friend, and I was the one who introduced her to Riley. If it hadn't been for me, they never would have done the dirty."

"That's ridiculous."

"Not according to Jonah," Gloria said. "And because I made that happen, it only followed that it was my fault that Riley was dead. After that Jonah fed and clothed me, and gave me a place to live, but I might as well have been one of the help."

"And you're blaming that on my *mother?*"

Gloria backed her slowly toward the bedroom doorway. "I told her not to have the baby, but she didn't listen to me. Said she was in love with Riley and wanted to bring his child into the world." She paused. "So I decided to spoil her fun."

Callie frowned. "What do you mean?"

"I started feeding her rat poison. Just little bits of it over the course of her pregnancy. I'd come over for sandwiches with her and your Nana Jean, and slip it into her iced tea."

Callie felt gut-punched.

Gloria had *murdered* her mother?

How was that possible?

She looked toward the bathroom and saw Harlan standing there now, wearing nothing but his jeans.

Gloria said, "No need to cover up on my account, Marshal. But I wouldn't advise you to go any farther."

Harlan didn't move.

"So where were we?" Gloria said to Callie. "Oh, right. Rat poison. Do you have any idea what it can do to a body?"

"I think I can figure it out."

"It has a little substance in it called warfarin. An anticoagulant. And if you give little doses to someone over a long period of time, the symptoms are minimal, but the cumulative effect is devastating, especially for a pregnant woman."

Callie understood. "The hemorrhaging. That's why she bled to death."

"The thing is," Gloria said, "you were supposed to die, too. And if it hadn't been for your grandmother's fast thinking, you would have. Right here in this room." She paused in the doorway. "I can't tell you how many times I thought about coming over here and putting a pillow over your face. My brother was gone, my father barely spoke to me, and I had every reason in the world to see you dead. But I couldn't get up the courage. A pillow isn't rat poison, and I knew if I tried, I'd probably wind up getting caught. And I didn't want that."

Callie nodded. "But now you have nothing to lose."

"Nothing at all," Gloria said. "It's all been taken away, thanks to—"

Callie hadn't prepared for it. The move was more instinctive than planned. Swinging a fist back, she slammed it into Gloria's wounded thigh.

Gloria grunted in pain and stumbled back—

Now Harlan was flying across the room toward them, launching into a tackle—

But Gloria recovered quickly, then raised

the gun and fired. The bullet hit Harlan in the shoulder and he went down hard onto the carpet as Callie turned and grabbed hold of Gloria's hand, trying to twist the gun away from her.

They struggled, stumbling sideways across the room, tumbling to the ground, Gloria grunting in pain again. But then she managed to break free from Callie's grip and swung the butt of the gun toward Callie's head, stunning her.

She scrambled away from Callie and got to her feet, holding her thigh with one hand as she turned the gun toward Callie.

"Nice try, but no cigar." Her finger brushed against the trigger. "Like I said, Cal, better late than nev—"

A gunshot rang out and Gloria froze in place, her eyes at first quizzical, then widening as she realized she'd been hit.

She looked down in surprise at the hole in her chest, then pitched forward, dead.

That was when Callie saw Nana Jean standing on the other side of the doorway, Grandpa's old World War Two revolver in her hand.

"That little witch killed my Mary."

Then she stared at the gun as if it were a foreign object, and dropped it to the floor.

Epilogue

No one mourned for Gloria. Jonah Pritchard refused to pay for her funeral, so she was buried in a pauper's plot at the city cemetery.

Megan Pritchard's trial was mercifully short, with minimal publicity—a near miracle in this day of electronic communications. She was found guilty of murder, kidnapping and conspiracy to commit murder and sentenced to life imprisonment at Wyoming State Penitentiary.

Sheriff's investigators took a closer look at the fire at Pritchard Ranch and came to the conclusion that Landry Bickham was the likely culprit, having set it to help make Gloria look like a victim. No one was ever sure who killed Billy Boy's partner, Brett, but at this point it didn't much matter.

Nobody saw much of Jonah Pritchard after that. He lived in seclusion at the newly built

Pritchard Ranch, surrounded by people who saw him as nothing more than a paycheck.

It was, Callie thought, a fitting punishment for man who had no soul.

Despite her initial shock, Nana Jean told Callie that she was sleeping better than ever at night, and would be around for a long time to come. And true enough, she seemed to have grown stronger over the months, her dizzy spells gone. And for reasons known only to Callie and Harlan, she stopped serving iced tea every afternoon.

Harlan recovered from his gunshot wound and he and Callie went down to Colorado Springs to pack up his apartment and move him to Williamson to live with her and Nana. Before leaving Colorado they stopped by the cemetery and laid flowers at Treacher's grave, quietly remembering his crooked smile, happy to have known him, if only for a short time.

At Sheriff Mercer's request, Harlan quit the Marshals Service and took a job with the Williamson County Sheriff's Office where an important vacancy had to be filled. A month later, Harlan got down on one knee and proposed to the only woman he had ever loved.

After nearly eight years on the job Callie took a leave of absence, planning to eat well and get plenty of exercise and sleep.

She was pregnant with their first child.

* * * * *

LARGER-PRINT BOOKS!
GET 2 FREE LARGER-PRINT NOVELS PLUS
2 FREE GIFTS!

Harlequin®

INTRIGUE®

BREATHTAKING ROMANTIC SUSPENSE

YES! Please send me 2 FREE LARGER-PRINT Harlequin Intrigue® novels and my 2 FREE gifts (gifts are worth about $10). After receiving them, if I don't wish to receive any more books, I can return the shipping statement marked "cancel." If I don't cancel, I will receive 6 brand-new novels every month and be billed just $5.24 per book in the U.S. or $5.99 per book in Canada. That's a saving of at least 13% off the cover price! It's quite a bargain! Shipping and handling is just 50¢ per book in the U.S. and 75¢ per book in Canada.* I understand that accepting the 2 free books and gifts places me under no obligation to buy anything. I can always return a shipment and cancel at any time. Even if I never buy another book, the two free books and gifts are mine to keep forever.

199/399 HDN FERE

Name	(PLEASE PRINT)	
Address		Apt. #
City	State/Prov.	Zip/Postal Code

Signature (if under 18, a parent or guardian must sign)

Mail to the **Reader Service**:
IN U.S.A.: P.O. Box 1867, Buffalo, NY 14240-1867
IN CANADA: P.O. Box 609, Fort Erie, Ontario L2A 5X3

Not valid for current subscribers to Harlequin Intrigue Larger-Print books.

**Are you a subscriber to Harlequin Intrigue books
and want to receive the larger-print edition?
Call 1-800-873-8635 today or visit www.ReaderService.com.**

* Terms and prices subject to change without notice. Prices do not include applicable taxes. Sales tax applicable in N.Y. Canadian residents will be charged applicable taxes. Offer not valid in Quebec. This offer is limited to one order per household. All orders subject to credit approval. Credit or debit balances in a customer's account(s) may be offset by any other outstanding balance owed by or to the customer. Please allow 4 to 6 weeks for delivery. Offer available while quantities last.

Your Privacy—The Reader Service is committed to protecting your privacy. Our Privacy Policy is available online at www.ReaderService.com or upon request from the Reader Service.

We make a portion of our mailing list available to reputable third parties that offer products we believe may interest you. If you prefer that we not exchange your name with third parties, or if you wish to clarify or modify your communication preferences, please visit us at www.ReaderService.com/consumerschoice or write to us at Reader Service Preference Service, P.O. Box 9062, Buffalo, NY 14269. Include your complete name and address.

HILP11B